# I'LL BE DAMNED

## A SHORT STORY COLLECTION BY

## SHANE RYAN STALEY

*[signature]*

### INTRODUCTION BY BRIAN KEENE

### ARTWORK BY R. S. CONNETT

*Eric -*
*Thanks for your*
*support!*
*— SRS*
*3/12/07*

DELIRIUM BOOKS

**FIRST EDITION**

**The following stories are reprinted by permission:**
"Tequila Son" © 2001 (originally appeared in *Terror Tales Online*)
"The Magic Cupboard" © 1999 (originally appeared in the chapbook *Burnt Offerings*)
"The Boy With The Razor-Sharp Teeth" © 1999
(originally appeared in the chapbook *Burnt Offerings*)
"Chocolate Jesus" © 2000 (originally appeared in the chapbook  *Chocolate Jesus*)
"Dysfunction" © 2000 (originally appeared in *Black Petals V.3 #3*)
"Road Kill" © 1998 (originally appeared in *Frightmares #3*)
"The Special Dish" © 1999 (originally appeared in the chapbook *Burnt Offerings*)
"Point of Interest" © 2000 (originally appeared in  the chapbook  *Sick Days*)
"The Dead Santa" © 2000 (originally appeared in  the chapbook  *Sick Days*)
"Bethlehem: 9 Months B.C." © 1999 (originally appeared in the chapbook *Burnt Offerings*)
"Caswell" © 1998 (originally appeared in *Outer Darkness #16*)
"The Smoker" © 2000 (originally appeared in the chapbook *Chocolate Jesus*)
"The Road Trip" © 1999 (originally appeared in the chapbook *Burnt Offerings*)
"Burnt Offering" © 1999 (originally appeared in the chapbook *Burnt Offerings*)
"The Mailman" © 1999 (originally appeared in the 1999 *Killer Frog Anthology*)
"The Ronnie Letters" © 2000 (originally appeared in the chapbook *Sick Days*)
"The Day Mr. Langford Cracked" © 1999
(originally appeared in the chapbook *Burnt Offerings*)
"The Golden Years" © 2000 (originally appeared in the 2000 *Killer Frog Contest* anthology,
placing runner-up in the short-short category)
"The Becoming" © 2000 (originally appeared in the chapbook *Chocolate Jesus*)
"Sick Day" © 2000 (originally appeared in the chapbook *Sick Days*)
"Shady Acres Church of God" © 2000 (originally appeared in *Delirium #2*)
"Twins" © 2001 (originally appeared online at  *Horrorfind.com*)
**The following material is printed here for the first time:**
"Introduction" © 2001 by Brian Keene
"Petey" © 2001 by Shane Ryan Staley
"Potty Mouth" © 2001 by Shane Ryan Staley
"Fallen" © 2001 by Shane Ryan Staley
"Opportunities" © 2001 by Shane Ryan Staley
"Bitchslapped" © 2001 by Shane Ryan Staley
"Worms" © 2001 by Shane Ryan Staley
"Blessed Is He Who Trusts In the Lard" © 2001 by Shane Ryan Staley

*I'll Be Damned*
Trade Paperback
ISBN 1-929653-28-X
All Stories © 2001 by Shane Ryan Staley
"Introduction" Copyright © 2001 by Brian Keene
Cover design and artwork © 2001 by R. S. Connett
Delirium Logo © 1999 by GAK
All rights reserved.

Delirium Books
P.O. Box 338
North Webster, IN 46555
E-mail: deliriumbooks@kconline.com
website: http://www.deliriumbooks.com
Copy Editors: John Everson and Bob Strauss

This book is dedicated to all those readers out there who continually buy my books and support my work. Without you, this just wouldn't be as much fun. Also, I'd like to thank my wife, Christi, for giving me the freedom to do this kind of thing. Your love has given me the drive to seek out my dreams and for that I am eternally grateful.

## SPECIAL THANKS

Shane Ryan Staley would like to thank the following people for their encouragement, contributions and overall support: **Brian Keene** (for the wicked introduction and for being "That Bastard"), **John Everson** (for being such a sick bastard/inspiration and for also copy editing this edition), **Bob Strauss** (who likes my stuff and who also copy edited this edition), **R. S. Connett** (easily the most talented artist/warped mind in all of the art world), **John Johnston** (a fan who lives down under), **Patrick Spencer** (who's just scary-lookin'!), **Gary Becht** (who has bought all my books and can't get enough perversion), **Lynn Colburn** (who just gives me a funny look when reading my books, but she still buys them), **Jessica "Hell" Smith** (the slutty cheerleader who still hasn't read all of *Chocolate Jesus* -- DAMN YOU, you Punk-Ass Bitch!), **Jessica's Mom** (who secretly loves my stories and just won't admit it), **Keith Waites** (the "so-called" mad bomber who I am not legally able to talk to anymore), **Carlton Mellick III** (where's my hoota-beast?), **Garrett Peck** (for the inspiration...though now he probably can't review this book since I mentioned his name), **Jim Lee** (ditto...I'm wiping out all the reviewers, dammit!), **Fredrick "Freddy" Barnsworth** (who hates me because he thinks I'm anti-gay...which brings a queer to my eye...I mean *tear*...), **Paige Haggard** (finally....a book that truly objectifies women...now you can rightfully bitch...), **Jeffrey Thomas** (how you like that one?), **Scott Thomas** (and your kinky chocolate-covered dwarf too...where the hell are my blonde virgins?), **Paul Tremblay** (who is my #1 Beeeeeaaaaaaach!), **Jesus Christ** (that guy owes me money!), **Satan** (for allowing me to keep my soul after I recruited a guy named Hodge who will surely give you the head you crave... and thanks for letting me keep the red sports car), and, finally, to all those who I forgot 'cuz I'm an asshole.

TABLE OF CONTENTS

# BETTER TO BURN

## AN INTRODUCTION BY BRIAN KEENE

Shane Ryan Staley is going to burn in hell.

No doubt about it. No room for argument or discussion.

The Devil's got a *special* place in mind for him...

Shane Ryan Staley makes up extreme horror stories and writes them down. Not a bad gig, considering that he could be a fry cook at McDonalds instead. But to say that Staley is simply a writer of hardcore horror is like saying that Dean Koontz and Richard Laymon have written "a few" books each. A big, frigging understatement in other words.

Is his fiction twisted? The answer is yes, and quite often it is also violent, gory, blasphemous, funny, and filled with so much over-the-top perversity and sex that Edward Lee's seminal hardcore novel *The Bighead* seems chaste by comparison. But there is something lurking beneath the gross-out imagery. As you peruse the stories in this collection, you'll find yourself enjoying them on two very different levels.

Obviously, there's the top layer of basic extremism. Staley's good at it, of this there is no doubt. He's quickly become one of the best in the business, ranking (in my opinion) alongside the likes of the maniacal Mark McLaughlin and the aforementioned Edward Lee.

Staley could have a career based on that talent alone. But peel away the outrageous and often hilarious trappings of his fiction, and his stories reveal a much deeper sub-texture. They're actually *about* something. They're about our world and the people we know—sick bastards that they are.

You've heard the expression 'through the glass darkly'? Forget that. The looking glass that Staley uses to view our world isn't just dark—it's fucking obsidian. What you call religion, he terms mind control. Where you see a prom queen, he sees a crack whore. Staley is a writer who focuses on the positive. He's positive that everything sucks.

There is much more to these stories than just a quick gross-out, my friends. There is the skewering of some sacred cows that desperately needed skewering. There is food for the funny bone and the blackened soul. There is a hidden wave of depth and emotion that will surprise you, sicken you, delight you and possibly even make you think.

There are some, no doubt, who will casually dismiss this collection as nothing more than the work of a misogynistic, antisocial hack. They'll liken it to a juvenile joke, scrawled crudely onto the bathroom stall.

What these literary snobs fail to realize however, is that quite often, the truth can be found in those humorous little bathroom ditties. Art is truth, and at their core, these stories are as blatantly true as it gets.

William S. Burroughs or Howard Stern, Shane Ryan Staley is a visionary. I rank him in the club whose departed members include Lenny Bruce, Philip K. Dick, John Lennon, Abbie Hoffman, and Sam Kinison. Every one of them was guilty of the same sin that Staley is guilty of. And according to society, every one of them went to hell.

Imagine *that* party in hell! That is a Hellfire Club I would love to belong to. It just may turn out that Shane Ryan Staley is taking us there. If that is the case, then I for one am along for the ride. I have been since I first encountered a story by him in a little zine called *Frightmares*. This was in the late '90s, back when we were both paying our dues in the zine culture. That first story made me a Shane Ryan Staley fan, and I've been on my way to hell ever since.

Now it's your turn. I just want to go on record as saying I warned you. If you turn the page, you're damned.

But then again, if you're going to go to hell, you might as well enjoy the ride.

And what a ride this one is...

Brian Keene
Baltimore, Maryland
June 2001

# TEQUILA SON

J ames shuffled his way through the crowd and situated himself at the bar. Smoke lingered like a faint wave of fog rolling past the pinball machines, over the television where WWF wrestling was displayed. He looked around the crowd, searching for a familiar face, but, instead, met eyes with a woman with long blonde-hair, in her early twenties, who smiled back. He had never seen her at the bar before and figured she was an out-of-towner or a first time visitor from the local college.

"What do you got, Mick? Anything new?" he asked the bartender.

Mick nodded. "Got a new import from Mexico. You up for it?"

"You know me," James said, "I'm the ultimate taste-tester!"

Mick uncapped a clear longneck bottle and slid it across the bar on a napkin.

James read the label: TEQUILA SON it stated in bold followed by the word "Light" outlined in white.

"Tequila in a beer bottle, huh?"

"Weird, eh?"

James read the ingredients, then swished around the bottle. Something pale in the bottle floated in the liquid along with debris.

"Wow, it's even got a big fucking worm in it."

"Look closer," Mick said.

James squinted, holding the bottle up to the dim lights. He swished the bottle around again and the pale grub-thing spun, drifted to the edge of the bottle, then sunk. As it turned again, James figured it was about an inch or two long, but then he saw the arms and legs.

"What the f—"

He tilted the bottle at a different angle and the thing floated up to the glass. He could see it was a tiny, pale man. It even had features such as a beard and indentations in its pale body replicating a robe.

"Jesus!"

"You got it," Mick said, laughing. "It's supposed to be Jesus all right!"

"Why?"

"Who knows. These imports always have some kind of gimmick to them. Anything to get people to drink their product."

Confused, James kept shaking the bottle, half-afraid to taste it.

"Maybe they took it from the old saying that you can't find Jesus at the bottom of a bottle. Hell, I don't know. Maybe they were trying to get religious people to drink it and collect the figurine."

"Has anyone else tried it?"

"You're the first. Go for it!"

James tipped the bottle and took a big gulp. The alcohol washed over his tongue, to the back of his throat. He swished what remained around in his mouth like a real connoisseur of alcohol. His taste buds exploded with remarkable flavor. The liquor was tangy, but not bitter and had no aftertaste whatsoever. He quickly took another swig and savored the exotic flavor.

"Damn, this is fucking divine!"

"Well, maybe you just uncovered the mystery then. That must be why the little wormy Jesus is in there!"

James smiled and chugged the rest until the Jesus figure stuck to the inside of the neck. He plucked it out with his finger and inspected it. It felt like a worm or a soggy noodle, but looked exactly like the Lord and Savior.

"You're not going to keep that, are you?"

"Hell no, that's where all the alcohol settles," he remarked, then popped the figure in his mouth and swallowed.

He felt lightheaded immediately. He felt the smile spreading across his face. His body felt calm and heavy as he looked around the room and suddenly caught a glimpse of the blonde approaching him.

"Hello," she said, "My name's Vicki."

"James," he said, trying to anchor down his smile before he looked like a jackass. "Have a seat."

Vicki looked at the seat and smiled, then bent close to his ear and whispered, "I thought more on the lines of going back to my place and fucking like mad."

James continued to stare down the low V-cut of her yellow blouse. Her well-tanned tits almost popped right out.

But for some reason, he didn't feel aroused. And before he could think about a clever reply, he blurted out, "No. I'm sorry, but that would be wrong. To lust is to sin. And I'm not married yet, so no sex for me."

Out of the corner of his eye he saw Mick's jaw drop.

The blonde looked disappointed, then embarrassed, then disgusted and departed without saying another word.

"What the hell are you doing? Are you fucking insane? She was hot!"

James glanced at Vicki returning to her table. Her tight blue jeans outlined her well-toned legs and ass. "Purity, my friend, it is your greatest possession."

Mick shook his head and ignored him the rest of the night.

The buzz wore off on the way home and James cursed out loud, "Am I fucking insane?"

He arrived at his apartment and paced the floor. *Okay,*

he thought, *I could be fucking some hot blonde right now with big tits and a nice ass. Why the hell didn't I take her up on it?*

He suddenly remembered the tequila and Jesus in it. It had to be the alcohol talking. Any other time, he would've jumped in the sack with any half-decent woman, just to get his rocks off.

He lurched toward the restroom, slid across the linoleum on his knees and threw up in the toilet. Portions of his lunch splattered the bowl, then the tiny worm-Jesus trickled out, plopping into the toilet.

******

The next night James sat at the bar and told Mick the whole story of why he had turned the woman down.

"Good thing. I thought you were turning gay on me or something."

"No, it had to be that drink. And that's the last time I'll try that stuff. It tasted so damn good, but it cost me a night of hot sex, so fuck that!"

"So try this," Mick said, uncapping another clear bottle. He sat it on the table in front of James.

James looked at the bottle and smiled. TEQUILA SON, the label read.

"Ha ha! Very funny."

"No, it's not the same. Look." Mick said, pointing again to the label.

James noticed the bottle was slightly different. It had black writing that read: *DARK*.

"*Tequila Son Dark*? Is there a Jesus in this one?"

"No."

"Good!"

James turned the bottle around, curious. He almost jumped back when he saw the snake coiled on the inside of the bottle. "Holy shit! How'd they get that fucker in there?"

Mick shrugged his shoulders. "Beats me. Must be about

ten inches long, but skinny as a worm. That must be why they only make these in longnecks! Anyway, it gives a new meaning to the concept of doing Snake Bites, huh?"

James couldn't help but smile. "Do you think this will do the opposite? Maybe I'll turn into a real party animal!"

"I think you're too late," Mick said, pointing across the bar.

James glanced across the heads of people, seeing Vicki at the same table, but with a man this time.

"It figures."

This time James slammed the whole drink in one gulp, the liquid stopping momentarily as the snake started squeezing its way out the top. James cringed, but started slurping at the snake like he would spaghetti, taking the whole thing in his mouth. He had to chew it up into three or four pieces before he could swallow and the scales grated the skin on the roof of his mouth. He felt his teeth sever muscle and vertebrae. The taste of ice-cold blood flooded his mouth, but he managed to engulf the whole thing without gagging. The last trickle of alcohol chased the snake and he sat back.

Everything around him seemed fast, suddenly alive with energy. Lights seemed brighter, the music louder. The women looked hotter and he felt suddenly very horny.

He looked back at the table where Vicki sat and cursed softly.

His face went numb minutes later and he felt blood racing through his body. His foot started tapping by its own freewill and he felt restrained to the seat.

He peeled himself off the barstool and approached Vicki. She gave him a dirty glare, which made him feel even more pissed than he already was. He looked at the man beside her, and said, "Excuse me, but I think I'll take your girlfriend for an hour or two."

It even surprised James, who was usually spineless when it came to confrontation.

The man stood, giving him a pathetic look. "Yeah right!"

James punched him the nose. The man stumbled back

SHAME RYAN STALEY / 13

and James wasted no time in dishing out an uppercut and kicking him in the balls. After the guy had hit the floor, James grabbed Vicki's arm and pulled her across the table, then forced her out of the bar and into his car.

"You could've just asked, you know," she said, adjusting her shirt. "I wasn't good enough for you last night!"

"Well tonight's another night and we're going to my place."

******

Before they even unmade the bed, James had already ripped off her clothes and tied her to the bedposts. Her luscious tits were well-rounded, her pink nipples hard and ready.

"Wow, you're kinky," she said, giggling.

James' cock was so much bigger than he ever remembered it being.

He lowered his face to her clit and began lapping. She pulled at the restraints and yelled, "Oh, oh yes, oh yes, eat me, eat me James!"

His tongue was still numb like his face, put he parted her lips with every forceful stroke of his tongue. Then he felt his stomach churn. He gripped her legs and felt sweat beading on his forehead. He turned to gauge the distance to the toilet, but knew he would never make it. He refocused on her vagina, a hole like a toilet, and he vomited.

"Are you okay?" she asked.

The slender snake somehow managed to come out in one piece. It flopped onto her pubic region then crawled inside her.

Again she pulled at the restraints, bucking her hips toward James. "Oh God, oh yes, lick me, oh, oh."

James just sat there, his dick shriveling.

She arched her hips wildly, for an hour, her eyes clenched tight, her wrists pulling at the handcuffs. James managed to get erect again just by watching her enjoyment. He even took his dick in his hand and started masturbating. Before long, he came all over her.

*At least I got something out of it*, James thought.

Vicki had already passed out. James checked to see if she was breathing and she was. Blood dripped from the handcuffs where they had cut into her wrists. He quickly unlocked them and wrapped her wrists with gauze.

He waited for the snake to come back out, but it never did.

\*\*\*\*\*\*

The next weekend, James returned to the bar, hoping to avoid Vicki.

"Dude, that's a wild story," Mick said. "So how much did you drink *after* you left here?"

"I'm dead serious! It never came out. I only had that one drink. I was sober, believe me!"

"I think a snake got in her all right. *Your* snake!"

Out of the corner of James' eye, he saw Vicki approaching.

She smiled, sat down next to him.

"Can I get you anything?" Mick asked her.

"No, I can't have anything," she replied.

Alarm bells went off in James' head.

"I need to talk to you, James. Privately."

*Oh shit*, James thought. *That's never a good thing.*

James walked with her outside the bar and she grabbed his hand.

"That was *sooo* wonderful last week. I can't even begin to explain it. You were so wonderful. You made me feel like I was on fire."

"Well, what can I say."

I was having orgasms all week, even after you were gone. It was incredible."

James just smiled, felt his face reddening.

"But I'm pregnant, James. I took a test and it was

positive."

The rest of the conversation James could only think about the snake, living somewhere deep inside her crotch.

******

"What the hell am I going to do, Mick?"

"Look," Mick cut in, "I think I know the answer."

James watched as Mick opened another bottle of *Tequila Son Light*, poured it in a glass, making sure the little Jesus fell in. He gave it to James.

"I'm not going to drink that shit. It's a little too late anyway, don't you think?"

"It's not for you, it's for Vicki."

"She won't drink it now that she's pregnant."

"She'll never know. You said it tastes like Kool-Aide."

James took a deep breath. "What do you think it will do to her?"

"I'm not sure, but it might just straighten her out."

James went over to Vicki and offered her the drink, claiming it was non-alcoholic. She sipped the drink and James waited patiently for her to drink down the little Jesus in the glass.

Finally she finished the drink off. And immediately demanded James to take her home.

During the drive, she said nothing. She just stared straight ahead.

James felt somewhat guilty for tricking her, especially when she exited the car without even saying goodbye. *Did she know it was alcohol?*

James headed back to the bar and couldn't help thinking about his misdeed. He pounded his fist on the dash and stopped the car. He could just keep driving and hope the whole incident would just blow over. If she was, in fact, pregnant, it couldn't be his. He didn't even have sex with her. She thought they had intercourse because James had jizzed all over her leg, and obviously, the way she walked later that next morning, the snake had done a number on her. But James never even put his dick near her after he had vomited the snake into her crotch.

But for some reason, James felt sorry for her. So he turned the car around and headed back to her apartment.

He knocked and no one answered. He tested the door and it opened. Two steps into the living room, James saw blood on the floor. A vase was broken against the wall. In the far corner, Vicki held a shard of the vase in her hand and was gouging her stomach.

"No!" James yelled, rushing at her.

"I must free myself from evil," she explained, then cut deeper. Blood gushed from the slit in her abdomen. James wrestled away the knife and put pressure on her stomach. Vicki broke down in tears, still struggling toward the jagged piece of porcelain.

Blood still squirted through James' fingers. He took his shirt off, applied more pressure.

Something suddenly bulged from the wound. James dropped his shirt and stepped back in shock.

The snake's pale head was sticking straight out of her abdomen, its head roaming back and forth in mid-air. It opened its mouth to hiss, but, instead, spit the little Jesus figure across the room, into the shag carpet.

It ducked back into the wound as Vicki fainted.

"Oh man," James said, "This can't be happening."

He knew he was in a predicament. She was obviously bleeding to death right before his eyes, but if he rushed her to the hospital, they would either discover the snake and think he implanted it there, or save the baby and reserve James the right to be a father, which he didn't want either. Or maybe the baby was already dead, and he could just take her to the hospital, then leave her for good. The possibilities were endless.

James finally acted, driving her to the hospital.

\*\*\*\*\*\*

# SHANE RYAN STALEY / 17

Three months passed. Vicki had been saved, though she had lost the baby, for which James was secretly glad. The snake had been extracted and the doctor's only explanation was that it was some kind of unknown parasite.

He still saw her from time to time at the bar, but they both managed to ignore each other.

Until one night, she was waiting by his car at closing time.

"Come back to my place. Just for old time's sake. Please."

James didn't mind the idea so much now that *Tequila Son* couldn't fuck things up. It would just be him and her, without that damn import Tequila to fuck everything up.

They were naked less than an hour later, rolling around on the bed. James could see the scars on her belly. That night three months prior kept slipping in and out of his mind.

"Come on, James. Give me the oral treatment. You were so good," she pleaded.

James knew she would be disappointed to learn that he wasn't responsible for the vaginal tongue-lashing previously, but he knelt just the same and started lapping away.

"Oh yeah, baby, give it to me good!"

James lapped harder.

"And say hello to the kids while you're down there."

Before it registered, a tiny head poked out of her vaginal lips. James almost licked it, before he pulled away and screamed.

As he stared, several more tiny heads poked through the darkness, their tongues flitting toward James.

"They're almost ready to come out now. They hatched last week. Isn't it wonderful."

James stared in disbelief. The only thought that went through his head other than fleeing was that he needed a drink. A *light* drink.

# PETEY

Bridgett knew she was in for a long night when she met the Robinsons and sensed they were escaping for the night instead of just going out. Mrs. Robinson's hair was a mess, she had dark circles under her eyes and limped awkwardly. Mr. Robinson seemed frightened by his own shadow, obviously hadn't shaved in weeks and didn't even look at his son on the way out the door. Strangely enough, he was limping too.

"Please, make sure he's in bed early. And please, *please* don't feed him after midnight. Make sure he doesn't trick you into giving him something."

"Oh, okay," Bridgett replied, wondering, *what the hell is he, a gremlin or something? What could possibly be so bad about one kid*?

\*\*\*\*\*\*

Bridgett had a flashback, to earlier in the day when her friend, Anne, had freaked out when she mentioned the Robinsons and their son.

"Oh my God, Bridgett, you're watching him overnight?"

"Well yeah, they said they would pay me one hundred dollars for the night. I don't usually make that much all month!"

"But it's Petey USM!"

"USM?  What does that mean?"

Anne looked around like someone was watching her.  "I can't talk.  He might hear me.  Just be careful and listen to their directions, okay?"

Before Bridgett could even say anything else, Anne ran off.

******

Petey just stared at her, smiling.

"So you're Petey, huh?"

Petey smiled wider.  "Yep," he said in a munchkin voice, "That's me!"

Petey looked like a normal toddler, short blonde hair, decked out in a small pair of blue jeans and a Helmo sweatshirt (Helmo being a little, scary red monster on the hit kids television show *Butternut Road*.)

Bridgett smirked.  "You like Helmo, huh?"

"Yep, he's the best."

"Have you ever seen *Helmo in Grumpland*?"

"Nope."

"How about we go rent it, would you like that?"

"Yep."

******

On the way to the video store, they walked by a man jogging with his dog.  The dog took one look at Petey and scampered off with its tail between its legs.

*That's odd*, Bridgett thought.

What was even odder was that the birds stirred violently in the trees.  Cats hissed in alleyways and an old priest crossed himself in passing.

They checked out the movie and headed home without further incident.

\*\*\*\*\*\*

**P**etey would not fall asleep. They watched *Helmo In Grumpland* eight times and midnight was fast approaching. She tried to call Anne on her cell phone, but no one answered, which was odd since she had a newborn to take care of. She and Billy, her boyfriend, had just brought the baby boy home from the hospital less than a month ago.

"Time for bed, Petey."

"Not tired."

Bridgett looked at the VCR clock. "Well, it's almost 11:45. It's late for little boys."

"I'm not little."

"Well, it's late for big boys too!"

"But I want more popcorn."

"Okay. One more bite and you promise you'll go to bed?"

"I promise."

Bridgett handed him the popcorn bowl and Petey smiled. And kept smiling.

Her wristwatch suddenly chimed.

She glanced back at the VCR which read 11:50.

"Oh, Jesus," she said, feeling her chest, trying to calm her rapid heartbeat.

She looked at her watch. Petey started crunching. Her watch read 12:01.

"What the h—" she said, looking over at Petey who chewed happily, playing with the VCR remote, changing the time.

"Oh no," she said, grabbing the bowl away from him, "Petey!"

He turned his head and smiled, his eyes suddenly dark and beady, his lips curling a little too far for his little face. "I'm the root of all that's evil, but you can call me Petey." His voice was much deeper, scratchier than usual.

Bridgett's hand was suddenly joined with Petey's little hand, both placed upon her chest. Petey cupped her breast, then squeezed.

"Petey, no! Bad!"

"No, it's good!" he yelled back, his voice sounding more like Barry White's than a child's.

He quickly jumped on her lap and straddled her. He pulled down her shirt and bra in one quick motion and latched onto her breast, sucking wildly. She pushed him away. "Feed me, feed me," he yelled in the childish, munchkin voice, then "Fuck me, fuck me," in a deep-pitched snarl.

His strength was overpowering. She tried to push him away, but he clung to her, then ripped off her shirt and bra. His hands were suddenly all over her, caressing her. He licked her nipples and she screamed for help. His hand worked its way down her blue jeans, into her underwear. His little fingers began banging away, forcing her legs to part. As he was focused down there, she reached for her cell phone and hit redial.

Meanwhile, Petey's tongue was working its way out of his mouth, dropping past his chest, slithering into her pants.

She screamed, noticing that it had grown well over a foot long already and showed no signs of stopping. It finally entered her clit just as Anne answered the phone.

"Anne? Help me!" she cried.

Petey's tongue rolled back into his mouth as he grabbed the phone.

"Yeah, come over here, bitch, so I can fuck you again," Petey yelled in the phone. All childishness had vanished from his voice. "You were a good babysitter! Nice and tight!"

"Get off me, Petey!" Bridgett yelled. "What is happening here?"

Petey said, "Why don't you tell her, Anne. Tell her what a good lover I am!" He then handed Bridgett the phone.

"What the hell is going on here?"

Anne was crying on the other end. "I'm so sorry, Bridgett. I tried to warn you, but I was afraid he might know and come and get me again."

"Who?"

"Petey USM"

"Why do you keep calling him that? What's USM mean?" The only thing Bridgett could think of was United States Marines, but that didn't make any sense.

Anne hesitated, then started bawling again. "It means Unstoppable Sex Machine. You fed him after midnight, didn't you?"

"He tricked me."

"I'm so sorry, Bridgett."

In the background, a baby screamed. Then Anne screamed and the line went dead.

And Petey pulled down his pants, revealing his skinny phallus that was fully erect and as long as his tongue had been just moments earlier.

"Oh my God, please don't—"

"Want to see something neat?"

"Anything, Petey," Bridgett sobbed, "Just don't hurt me."

"Okay, watch!"

Suddenly red hairs sprouted all over his face. His long blonde locks turned curly and red. His eyes bulged, moving to the top of his head. His mouth cracked, turning black inside and stretching from ear to ear.

He had somehow mutated into a life-size well-hung Helmo.

"Are you ready to play," he said, in a girlish Helmo voice.

"La-la-la-la   La-la-la-la   Helmo's Land!" he shouted. "Welcome to Helmo's Land, Bridgett. Time to play! Let's play Helmo in *Humpland*!"

And the rest was just an extension of the nightmare. His cock was red and hairy as he ripped off her pants and panties and entered her. She fought with all her strength, but could only lay there, pinned under the furry red creature with an oversized penis, pumping in and out of her at lightning speeds.

The night lasted forever as Bridgett fell in and out of consciousness. Sometimes she would waken to the furry cock in her mouth, in her cunt and up her ass. Once it was even under her armpit and several times between her breasts. She felt sticky, then noticed that every time the Petey-Helmo-thing came, black sludge shot from its dick.

****** 

The Robinsons came home the next morning.

Bridgett lay sprawled naked on the couch with tiny Petey nestled on the floor, snoring away innocently.

"Oh my God, Jim," Mrs. Robinson said, gasping, "It happened again!"

"Shit! Why can't these damn teenage girls listen to directions? You told her not to feed him after midnight, right?"

Mrs. Robinson rolled her eyes, nodded.

Bridgett rose, stumbled forward, feeling weak and exhausted.

Black cum dripped from her belly, her crotch and her hair. Her mouth was dry and sticky; a bad taste lingered like licorice dipped in rotten meat sauce. Her ass felt like a giant gaping hole. Her crotch was numb.

She slowly slipped on her panties and jeans and what remained of her blouse.

Mr. Robinson threw a one hundred-dollar bill on the couch beside her as well as a pill wrapped in cellophane.

"Morning after pill. It would be wise to take it. You don't want to end up like one of our *old* babysitters. Evil seeds breed nothing but evil. I should know," he said, rolling up his sleeve. He held his arm in front of Bridgett and she witnessed his hairs turning red for a split second. He smiled. "But Petey is so much worse than I ever was!"

Bridgett took the money and pill and limped out the door.

"And by the way," Mrs. Robinson said, peeking her head out of the doorway, "You breathe a word of this to anyone and he'll find you. You can't hide from Petey. There's nowhere safe, believe us."

# THE MAGIC CUPBOARD

Andy peered down at the tiny blood stains scattered around his room. Ten minutes before his mother had swept, there had been hundreds of tiny soldiers and Indians, mostly corpses, strung across the shag carpeting. Some had been scalped, others shot with arrows and bullets or stabbed. The few that were still alive perished with the rest as his mother sucked them up in the sweeper.

Andy liked watching things die. That was the best thing about the magic cupboard. It had the power to bring things to life, so Andy could stomp on them or burn them with lighters. It had only been a normal cupboard until he took it to the strange hermit who lived down the road. Andy asked him to put a spell on the cupboard in order to make it like the one he had once seen in a movie. And the strange man had worked wonders on the oak cupboard. It was definitely Andy's new favorite toy.

Andy sifted through the rest of his toys, looking for more toy soldiers or Indians to put in the magic cupboard. But all he had left was trucks and cars, balls and puzzles — nothing that would come alive.

Andy moved into his sister's room and searched the premises while she slept. He quietly pulled a Barbie and a Ken doll from the wreckage. Returning to his room, he placed both in the magic cupboard, shut the door, and reopened it.

Barbie strutted out on the arm of Ken and they proceeded to climb up the bed sheets, disappearing underneath.

"That sucked," Andy whispered to himself.

Beneath the bed sheets, he suddenly heard a woman's scream.

"Yes, he's killing her!" Andy said as he pulled back the sheets to find a miniature bra and panties shoved beneath the pillow. Farther down, inside the sheets, he heard moaning and a woman's voice cry out, "Oh yes, Ken, harder, harder!!! Give it to me big guy!"

Andy threw down the covers, picked up a tennis racquet and smacked every square inch of his bed, finally hearing tiny bones breaking beneath the strings.

Next he tried his older brother's room. He crept in unnoticed, half-scared at what he might find. Pictures of skulls and strange-looking men with guitars wearing dark leather pants were plastered on posters, wallpapering his entire room. On the bookshelf was a strange ceramic statue of some person wearing a black-hooded outfit, his or her face lost in shadow. On the base of the statue were the words *Grim Reaper*.

Andy stuffed the statue in his pocket and returned to his room. Once there, he placed the statue in the magic cupboard and opened the door. The dark-hooded figure leapt out and ran out the door, into the hallway. Andy followed, tracking him into the storage room. As Andy turned the corner, he saw the figure lunge into the cat litter box, atop Fluffy's back. Fluffy hissed and ran into a corner.

The dark, faceless figure chanted, waving its bony fingers into the air.

Fluffy dropped dead. The figure jumped off and ran out of the room.

Andy poked at Fluffy with a dust mop, but the cat's body was hard and stiff.

Down the hall, he heard his sister scream. Something heavy hit the floor.

Andy quickly placed Fluffy back into the litter box to avoid getting blamed for his death and went to his sister's room to investigate. He peeked into the dark room and watched as her body was slowly dragged beneath the bed.

Andy shut the door and set his sights on his parents room. As he scanned their room, he found nothing of interest that could be brought back to life until he saw the miniature half-naked man hanging on a wooden cross on the wall above the bed.

He opened the magic cupboard and shoved the crucifix in. He looked closer at the man spread upon the wooden cross. He shut the door and reopened it.

Andy jumped back and quickly covered his ears to the shrill screams of the man. Blood dripped from the man's wrists and feet which remained nailed to the crosspiece. The tiny man wriggled, trying to free himself to no avail.

The monotonous piercing scream echoed around his room. Andy stepped outside and shut the door. He walked downstairs to where his father was fixing himself a sandwich.

"Hey there, sport. Seen your sister lately?"

Andy shook his head.

"It's not like her to stay in bed this long."

"Dad," Andy said, sitting next to him at the table. "There's a tiny man in my room and he's screaming."

His father chuckled. "Oh really."

"Yeah," Andy said, "He's really annoying me."

His father looked him in the eye. "Have you thought about flushing him down the toilet?"

Andy shook his head and smiled. "No, but that would work!"

His father laughed. "You and your imagination!"

Andy opened his bedroom door and wrapped a towel over the man on the cross to muffle his screams. He moved to the bathroom and pried at the cross, detaching the man's body. He then dropped the man in the toilet and flushed. Bubbles from his screams arose as his body swirled around the bowl, finally sucked under, soon disappearing.

Andy sighed, relieved to hear silence.

He turned toward the doorway, to search for the hooded figure again. He felt an eerie sensation, leaving the figure running abroad. It felt almost like there was a rat loose in the house. Andy didn't want to wake up at night and have to worry about the dark hooded figure lurking beneath his bed.

So he set mouse traps in the kitchen and bedrooms. He sprinkled rat poison under the cupboards and sinks, behind furniture and appliances.

As he climbed the stairs to his room, he caught sight of his brother's door cracked open and loud droning heavy metal music echoing from the speakers. He peeked in, seeing his brother's body draped over a chair, the tiny hooded figure setting flames to his hair. The dark figure again chanted and waved its bony arms, summoning death. Smoke from the incense swirled around the figure as it probed its staff into Andy's brother's head.

Andy grabbed a guitar and smashed it over the tiny shadow-enshrouded figure. A tiny black grease spot spewed atop his brother's head.

Andy sighed, knowing it was about time to get rid of the magic cupboard. It had turned into more work than fun, plus he had run out of things to bring back to life. And he had a funny notion that if he did find things to bring to life, he would now have a hard time killing them.

Next he would beg the strange hermit to make him a life-size talking doll that looked like his sister. Andy wondered if the strange man could construct such a thing before his parents realized what had happened. He knew it was his only hope since her body was far too large to stuff into the magic cupboard. *At least if it was all in one piece...*

# THE BOY WITH THE RAZOR-SHARP TEETH

E very smile seemed dangerous with pointed teeth and bleeding gums. And with dark beady eyes and breath that could choke a mule, no one ever talked to the boy with razor sharp teeth.

His deformity was so evident that his name became "The Boy With The Razor-Sharp Teeth." Even Ms. Adams addressed him as such ever since the morning he first arrived during show and tell.

Jimmy Wilson had just finished showing off his new wooden rubber band gun by flipping Jackie in the rear. Ms. Adams jerked the gun away from him as The Boy With the Razor-Sharp Teeth entered.

I looked in the doorway and there was the hideous smile. Susie and Jenny screamed, Ms. Adams gasped, holding her chest. Jimmy Wilson looked up, shouted "What the F—" before his jaw dropped.

The boy quickly shut his mouth, looked down into the rust-colored carpeting and swayed back and forth with some mutated innocence.

"You must be Daniel," Ms. Adams deduced, finally

collecting herself, though her face still slightly cringed. "Come sit in the circle....we're in the middle of show-and-tell."

The boy shuffled over next to me and crossed his legs. A sour, rotten smell drifted from his gaping mouth. The girls shifted away.

"Okay, I believe it's Sarah's turn. What do you have for us today?"

Sarah Weller opened the cardboard box in front of her as Jake Foster probed the holes poked through each side.

Something squealed inside until she pulled out a fat rodent.

"This is my Guinea Pig, Virgil."

Ms. Adams smiled. "Class, let's all welcome Virgil to his first day at school."

Everyone sat in silence, staring at The Boy With the Razor-Sharp Teeth.

"Pass him around, Sarah!"

As the Pig moved counter clockwise it dropped a pile on Liz's forearm, chewed a hole in Brandon's shirt pocket, and crawled up Megan's dress. The pig wriggled in Jake's hands until he reluctantly handed it to The Boy With the Razor-Sharp Teeth. The Guinea Pig glared up at the boy, unmoving, like it too was terrified. The Boy With the Razor-Sharp Teeth studied it closely, like it was the first animal he had ever seen, softly stroking its head.

Then he popped the Guinea Pig in his mouth and started chewing.

Everyone rose, scurrying away. The girls screamed, the boys looked on in astonishment. Ms. Adams passed out cold.

The terrible squeals surfaced, muffled within the grinding cavity. Blood spilled from his lips, streaming down his shirt. Bones snapped, the animal shook violently. The boy's death grip soon took the animal's life. Somebody vomited down my trousers.

Soon the boy belched and the room cleared.

About a week later, The Boy With the Razor-Sharp Teeth

came back. Sitting in the back row, he was ignored. He became a loner, unspoken to and untouched by everyone. Soon his hideous face turned sad and lonely.

I felt sorry for the boy. Being a loner myself, I knew the emptiness he must have felt. Ms. Adams must have felt the same way I did because soon she found ways to force him to interact with the rest of the class, though he never made an effort by himself.

But, with his lack of effort, it never made a difference. In a game of dodge ball, all the boys aimed directly at him, hoping to knock out a tooth in order to claim a souvenir. Billy Ripley came close, striking the boy on the side of the face. But the ball just stuck there, deflating on a tooth which was poking through the boy's cheek.

When he slept during nap time, kids would throw things into his mouth just to see if he would chew them up. It started out with pencils, crayons, and erasers and progressed to pencil sharpeners, gym shoes, and glue bottles.

His one moment of glory was when everyone in the cafeteria gathered around him to watch an entire tray of corndogs being devoured, sticks and all.

He proved to me a number of things that day: the boy wanted to be liked, he needed to be accepted, and that cafeteria corndogs were actually digestible.

His face started turning grey and weary, always looking downward. He always kept his mouth shut, never even smiled or yawned. It was as if his difference kept him from opening up to the others. Months had passed and he made no effort to fit in.

Show-and-tell rolled around week after week and he sat there, saying and showing us nothing about himself.

Until one day.

To the class's surprise, he answered Ms. Adam's request with a jagged, horrible smile, looked around and spoke for the very first time.

"I want to show everyone something."

"Go right ahead, Daniel."

He pulled out a small box with a collection of both plastic and glass bottles.

"What do you have to share with us?"

He faintly smiled, uncapped a liquid-filled bottle and began sprinkling it over everyone.

Girls giggled and boys smeared the substance on one another.

"Daniel, you're making a mess. Please stop it!"

The Boy With the Razor-Sharp Teeth continued relentlessly dousing his peers in liquids and powders and other substances.

A glass bottled rolled against my leg. I hesitated to touch it, frightened that it might be some form of potion which would mutate everyone into People With Razor-Sharp Teeth. Finally I mustered the nerve to flip the bottle over and read the label.

Suddenly Jenny and Susie screamed. Liquids and sandlike granules with an eye-watering fragrance pelted my arm. Crimson splashed against my shirt, running down atop the bottle of meat tenderizer I held tightly. It took what seemed minutes to be brave enough to look up toward the screams.

Susie's legs were missing and Tony's face was half-eaten. Bobby crawled toward the door, dragging behind him a mass leaking from his punctured stomach.

The door slammed shut. Dark, beady eyes glared at me, but lunged in another direction, to where Ms. Adams stood, breaking a window with an umbrella. The Boy With the Razor-Sharp Teeth came down on her, sinking his mouth into her neck, ripping out a segment of her spine. She flopped wildly against the heat register, her body trembling in shock.

There was a disturbance at the door, a few more screams, distant sirens closing in.

I crawled into a corner and sat there, witnessing the boy returning to the wounded to devour what remained.

Even when the police arrived, the horror of what they saw

repelled them from the door. No shots were fired, no dogs came barging in. Just Daniel, the boy with the razor-sharp teeth, and I glaring face to face, surrounded by fresh carnage and crimson-stained carpeting between blood-splattered walls.

Slowly, his dark beady eyes gazed over to a bottle next to me. He picked up the bottle and serenaded me with tenderizer like a priest exorcising demons with holy water. He smiled and I saw flesh caked against his gums and an entire fingernail stuck in a gap between two pointed teeth.

In the back of my mind, the screams of my classmates echoed as well as their taunts and name-calling, their cold shoulders, and nasty glares.

And I understood him. And he, in turn, saw this in my eyes and stopped.

A tear streamed down his face in a pink line, separating two congruent segments of his own blood-caked cheek.

"But they were never mean to you just because you were different and they were normal," he whispered sadly, his eyebrows arched, searching to understand. "They accepted you."

I shook my head and looked away in frustration. "You never let them know you. You never gave them a chance to accept—"

"No!" he shouted. "They would've always seen me as the different one."

"It is true you have something strange," I mumbled, feeling the anger bubbling within my mouth, my cheeks expanding with every passing minute. "You have something that they don't, but if you would've let yourself get to know them better you would've learned that Susie has a third nipple and Billy has a glass eye. Megan has no genitals and Liz's really a guy. Jake's heart is on the outside of his chest and Jimmy thinks he's a tree. Brandon talks to demons and Ms. Adams is part turkey. And I can't forget Sarah, poor Sarah, possessed by the ghost of Hitler, nor Jenny having sold her soul for cash. Jackie is a seven-year-old stripper and

Bobby is living with a deadly rash. Tony collects chicken heads and Denny lives in a hole. Candy has sex with aliens and Marvin is really a troll."

"Ms. Adams...part turkey?"

"Fears Thanksgiving and gobbles from time to time."

"But I didn't know..I'm so sorry."

My heart spasmed wildly within my chest, sweat trickled down my forehead. My jaw cracked. "Didn't your parents explain why they put you in this class? And that it was a special class..."

"B-but what about you? You're normal!"

I gagged, feeling the anger escape me. My tongue lashed at him. His eyes fluttered in horror as he watched my tongue uncoil and branch into two flickering points which quickly wrapped around his neck and squeezed.

# POTTY MOUTH

"You don't know Jesus, that's your problem!"

It was the first thing the bitch ever said to me. I had been working with her for over a week and knew it was coming. It was evident just by looking at her. She had her hair curled into a tight bun and sported black-rimmed glasses. Even despite her looks, what other person would show up for work with a framed picture of Jesus to mount at her workstation? The first time I looked at it, I thought it was her kid or something, but I should've known better – no man on earth would want to fuck, let alone impregnate, a woman like that. She probably had a time limit in which she could enjoy sex only in the missionary position, only to hold a candlelight vigil to repent after her orgasm.

Okay, so I hated the bitch the first time I laid eyes on her, but what was she to get into my business?

So I cussed a little every time the machine fucked up or swore at the clock and shook my head when time dragged. That's what factory life does to a person.

She repeated herself after I pretended not to hear. "Your problem is that you don't have Jesus in your life."

I peered over and saw the gold cross dangling from her neck. She had cross earrings too. Her shirt was a plain gold color with (you guessed it) a cross with the words HE DIED FOR YOU beneath it. She had a ring on with a gold cross and a button on her jacket with a cross. The only way I could relate to all this was that I was getting pretty goddamn *cross* myself about then.

"Yeah, I know Jesus," I replied, "I met him at the bar last night. Quiet Mexican – drinks Tequila. Gets shit-faced fast and grabs all the waitresses asses!"

"Oh my," she said, sounding more like June Cleaver than anyone I've ever heard before. "You ought to be ashamed of yourself, son. You have a demon in you, that's for sure. Always swearing and taking the good Lord's name in vane. That's what demons do, they wait until your soul is wounded and then climb aboard!"

"Uh huh," I said, trying to contain my smirk.

"There's the demon of hate which you have. There are also demons of lust and greed and –"

"Uh oh," I said, "Looks like you got stuck with the Ugly demon."

She looked at me strangely, like she didn't understand.

"Okay, maybe the demon of Stupidity."

Her face turned red and she turned back to her machine and started working.

******

I wish I could say that was the last of our confrontations, but I couldn't be that lucky. The next day, she placed a Bible beside my workbench, smiled really big and said, "The answers are in here."

I used it as a coaster to set my pop can on.

"Sinner," she scowled.

"Bitch," I muttered.

******

"God damn piece of fucking shit!" I yelled as the machine broke down for the third time that afternoon.

"You need to exercise that demon in you," she said,

I'LL BE DAMMED | 36

watching my tantrum. "You're a plain and simple potty mouth and it's because you have the demon of hate inside you."

"Lady," I said, turning toward her, "Bite me!"

"Is there a problem here," the supervisor, Rick, cut in.

"Yes there is. This woman won't leave me alone."

"He keeps taking the Lord's name in vain," she said, "He's the worst potty mouth I ever heard."

"Please," Rick said, "Keep your comments to yourself. And Connie, mind your own business. Just because this man's a sinner doesn't mean you have to try and save him. Some people are just meant to burn in hell."

It was at that moment when I noticed the cross pin on his bow tie.

******

Later that night, I went to the library and studied demon possessions and the Christian beliefs concerning the phenomena. I surfed through the rites for exorcism and a bunch of related topics. Finally, after clearing the Biblical references from my desk, I wandered upon a yoga-like exercise that was said to clear one's soul of demons. I read the entire article since it was more new age than Biblical mumbo-jumbo. For some reason, it really interested me. And gave me a great idea as well.

******

The next day the war continued. I wore my Ministry t-shirt with their popular song title on it: JESUS BUILT MY HOTROD. Connie noticed it instantly.

"Take that shirt off now!"

I just smiled and continued to work. "Sorry but I'm busy now. Maybe some other time. And isn't there a sexual harassment policy here?" I asked. "You better control your hormones. Just because you haven't been laid since high school doesn't mean you have to proposition me to take off my shirt."

Her face was already fire-red. She dropped her tools and marched straight into my workstation. "YOU listen here. You are the lowest-life sinner I have ever seen. You are a disgrace to God's good name. You—"

She suddenly waved to the supervisor and he rolled his eyes, coming straight to the scene that was unfolding.

"Make him take that shirt off."

Rick looked seriously at the shirt. "Yes, please take that off."

"No way!"

"It's obviously disrupting the work environment. Take it off!"

Just as I planned.

Rick ducked into an office and came back, handing me a company T-shirt. He smirked, then walked off. I turned to Connie and slowly peeled the Ministry shirt off. She watched with pure satisfaction until she saw the words I had scrawled on my chest prior to work.

JESUS BLOWS GOATS.

She gasped out loud and I prepared for the worst. I started to breathe deeply and focus all my energy onto pure, simple things, drowning her out completely, though in my mind I could still make out her incessant ramblings.

"HE died on the cross for your sins. You are the devil's own pride and joy. You are nothing but trash, you sorry son of a bitch! You..."

The whole factory suddenly turned, looking in her direction.

"...I wish you would die right now and I could watch you burn in eternal hellfire. I hate you..."

The word "hate" reverberated in my mind, not from her insult, but for my own meditational purposes.

And then it started to happen. I exhaled deeply and felt my body pushing something out. It felt like all the carbon dioxide was slowly being replaced by the freshest oxygen, cleansing me, rejuvenating me.

I suddenly lost my breath, my eyes shot open, and I witnessed a slight frosty mist exiting my mouth. It was the same type of smoky air you exhale on cold winter days outside, but it was over seventy degrees in the factory. I looked closely because it was so faint that no one else would be able to make it out unless they were looking directly at it. And once I identified the outline, I could only laugh. For there before me, floating in mid-air, was the demon of hate, shrouded in an almost invisible mist. Its eyes were wicked and probing, its jagged mouth snarling into a smile. Its head was huge above a body that seemed more like a faint thundercloud eclipsing the air.

It took one look at Connie, then dove straight into her mouth.

It quickly disappeared into her body, as her ranting died down to its final words, "You stupid loser!"

The rest of the night she remained strangely silent.

\*\*\*\*\*\*

Life was never the same after that day. It felt like a hundred-pound weight had been lifted off my shoulders. I felt myself smiling. Nothing seemed to bother me. Especially Connie and her endless cussing and bitching about everything under the sun.

Within weeks, she took up smoking. Coworkers said she started barhopping on the weekends and frequenting male strip clubs during the week after work. I noticed all her cross attire slowly diminished to ripped-up jeans and concert t-shirts. She wore tight-fitting tank tops and got a tattoo of a barbed wire rose.

She was actually looking pretty damn hot. Especially after letting her hair down and no longer wearing bras to work.

One day after my machine broke down I calmly knocked on Rick's office and opened the door. He scrambled briefly, then froze as Connie, with her hair wild and flowing down her back, was on her knees, giving him head. And she didn't even stop when I entered. She just continued to bob up and down, licking his balls and kneading his shaft. There was this huge smile on her face that even made me smile.

Because I knew.

Hate had invited some friends.

# CHOCOLATE JESUS

S unday school was no place to be on a gorgeous summer day. Ms. Larson would rattle on about how Jesus did this and Jesus did that and how everybody was going to burn in hell if they didn't live their lives like snobby little pricks who judge everyone else.

Alex hated church. His mother forked over five bucks each Sunday for him to put in the collection plate, but, instead, he'd hike on over to Louie's candy store and buy himself an assortment of candies and chocolates.

His mother never knew. She was always wrapped up with Nick. Though the guy was half her age, she hung all over him like he was the last guy on earth. She stopped going to church altogether and started getting on her knees for other things instead.

Alex kicked up a cloud of dirt down the alleyway as he stared back at his house. The shingles on the roof whistled in the wind and the gutters were filled with plant life. Things had gone from bad to worse since his father had been killed in a car wreck almost two years ago.

And that's why he hated church so much. If Jesus really existed, then his father would never have died so young. How could someone so powerful and good let something so bad happen? Preacher Roberts had said that everything happens for a reason and when Alex asked why, the preacher simply shrugged his shoulders and patted him on the head.

That was the last time he attended.

As always, Alex arrived at the candy store and purchased a chocolate bar with the collection money his mom had sent with him. He sat on a park bench outside the store and watched Sunday-goers pass along the street. He leaned back on the bench and let the warm sun cascade down his arms and face. He closed his eyes and drifted to sleep.

By the time he awoke, the sun had melted his chocolate to the park bench. Alex noticed its shape had distorted in the heat in a strange way. And Alex almost pissed his pants as he looked upon a tiny figure of Jesus staring back with chocolate eyes.

Alex rubbed his eyes and shook his head, as if the motion might knock him from a deep slumber and a fitful dream. But the chocolate figure only crossed his arms and waited silently.

The figure's face was sculpted almost perfectly as in the various portraits his mom had hung across her bedroom walls. With the same beard and pleading, gentle eyes, this figure sported a wavy robe and sandals just like Alex would have pictured Him wearing.

"Tell me your troubles, my son," the figure spoke clearly, as if the sound had been transported from some insane puppet master, channeling the speech solely into Alex's ears.

Alex stuttered, then shifted to the other side of the park bench, trying to ignore the strange little man made of pure chocolate.

"Don't be afraid, Alex. I am the light of the world, remember?"

Alex glanced around, afraid that someone might walk by and see him talking to a half-foot chocolate fudge chunk that resembled the Lord. "Go away...leave me alone!"

"Your soul must go on, Alex. You mustn't skip church and indulge yourself with pleasure over obedience," Jesus said. "The key to unlocking heaven's gate is discipline and sacrifice."

"I don't want to talk to you."

"Your father wants you to go to church and live a life that's righteous."

Alex perked up, feeling saddened, but yet aware of the newfound possibility. "I want to talk to him. I miss him!"

The chocolate Jesus smiled and held out his tiny hands, palms up. The chocolate slowly melted and bubbled, shifting and coalescing into a broad-shouldered man with a mustache and glasses.

"Dad!"

His father lifted his chocolate hand and waved. "Hi son!"

Alex pouted. "You're not really my dad."

The chocolate figure crossed his arms and said, "It's me, Alexander. I'm in heaven now."

Alex felt a wave of disappointment, considering his father was once warm flesh that could be hugged or able to play catch with in the back yard. Now, after his death, he was reduced to appearing as a chocolate chunk, only because Jesus had allowed him to. What kind of a deal was that?

The figure responded to Alex's disinterest by morphing back into the Jesus figure. "I know you're mad and don't understand. You're young and you have to learn that all things happen for a reason, but in the end, you'll be rewarded in the kingdom of heaven."

Alex felt his lip quiver. He thought about the last day he had seen his father and how much his life had changed since he had died. He thought about his mom and how she had changed too. She never cooked meals and hardly spent time with Alex. It was as if Alex only reminded her of his father, and she couldn't stand the pain of being alone, to where she had picked up Nick to fill the space. And Nick, in turn, lived off his mother and when the walls were quiet in their room, he'd secretly sneak over to Alex's and talk to him softly while slipping his hands under the sheets, touching Alex in a way that no one else ever had. And Alex felt bad, like he had lost his place in the world. At age ten, he felt as if he didn't belong. He trusted no one, not even the tiny figure which stared back with pleading, gentle eyes.

"Please listen—"

"No!" Alex shouted, leaping from the park bench. "You listen, for a change. Every night I talk to you and you *don't* listen. You don't protect me from Nick. But you allowed my father to die and leave me here alone."

"But nothing matters down here..."

"Bullshit!" Alex knelt closer to the tiny chocolate deity. "Everything matters. The world is bad and everyone down here is losing hope. No one can see heaven from down here anymore."

"But it's the people who have tainted this world," Chocolate Jesus explained.

"But it was God who created this world in the beginning. And when He did, He created the bad as well. He created things that made Dad leave me and He made things like Nick."

"But I've finally come to help you, Alex."

Alex felt rage. He felt how his swollen rectum still burned from Nick's last visit. He felt loneliness and distrust. "Well, you've come too late."

Alex picked up the chocolate Jesus and shoved him into his mouth.

He clamped his jaws shut over a tiny scream and chewed with delight. He felt movement in his mouth slowly dwindle to an oozing layer he licked off his teeth and gums. The chocolate tasted so...divine.

******

Alex returned home to find Nick snoring on the couch and a note from his mother that read: *Alex – went to the grocery. Fix Nick something to eat when you get home.*

Alex felt his stomach cramp from eating the whole chocolate chunk on an empty stomach. He ran to the bathroom, pulled down his pants, and released his bowels into the toilet. Sweat trickled on his forehead as he strained.

Before he could reach for the toilet paper, Alex felt something splashing in the toilet, clinging to his butt. An echo of a gurgle erupted as he leaned forward.

Peering at his behind, Alex gasped, seeing a tiny lumpy figure still sprouting from his excrement. The oblong turd shifted as arms molded onto each side followed by legs. The tapered point of the mass fell off into the water as a horned head suddenly formed with a face that smiled. The pointed tail was the last thing that developed.

The figure used its newly formed hands to spread apart Alex's butt cheeks. In a gravelly voice, the figure muttered, "Damn, kid, he sure did a number on you, huh?"

Alex felt his face flush at the embarrassing fact. He felt weak and worthless.

The figure slowly left the area, climbing up his back and onto his shoulder, leaving a wet trail of footprints in its path. "How about we make your world a little brighter today?" the devil asked.

Alex shrugged his shoulder by mistake, smashing the turd-figure into his neck. "How can we do that?"

He felt the figure slowly regenerate into its natural (or unnatural) shape and, for the first time, he noticed the unpleasant aroma that emanated from the creature. He glanced to the side and noticed that the devil had two pieces of corn for eyes and chunks of sunflower seeds for ears.

"We're going to have some fun, kid," the devil stated, speaking from the depths of a cavity comprised of a hollowed popcorn kernel.

"How's that?"

"Let's play three wishes," the devil said, "What's your first?"

"I want my dad back," Alex blurted out.

The dark lump of a head shifted back and forth, sadly. "Nope, sorry kid. Jesus already killed your dad off. Next wish."

Alex's frown suddenly turned into a slight smile. "My

second wish is to watch Nick suffer and my third is to watch him die."

"Now that I can do!" the lopsided mass of excrement grinned. "We're going to make ol' Nick a sandwich. My favorite is bologna, with Miracle Whip, pickles and razor blades. Add a dash of Draino here and there and you got a power lunch."

Alex's smile widened, feeling his loneliness suddenly fading. "I think I'm going to like you."

"I thought you would."

# DYSFUNCTION

O fficer Dan Callahan pulled the trigger and the bullet ripped through the man's skull. The figure fell back into darkness as a scream echoed above the chaos.

"Hold your fire! There's still somebody in there!" Dan yelled across the yard. Fellow police officers were scattered across the lawn, some behind trees, others kneeling behind the doors to their cruisers, guns aimed toward the darkened house.

Dan ran up to the door and peeked inside. A young girl squatted next to the man's body which was sprawled across the tiled floor, blood oozing through the back of his head, his body still twitching.

"Get back, sweetie. It's okay. Come here."

The girl stared at Dan silently, a hollow gaze etched solidly into her face.

Dan stepped in through the shattered glass of the front door. The elder couple who owned the house were on the kitchen floor, hands and feet bound, throats slashed. Their blood pooled together in a stream which disappeared beneath the refrigerator.

Dan listened over his own heavy breathing, but heard no other movements. The girl watched him as he moved closer, scanning him like he was some kind of prey stumbling blindly towards her. Dan shivered as this eerie feeling momentarily eclipsed everything including the danger of another intruder waiting in the shadows. He continued, keeping his eyes on the dead assailant whose body still shifted and quivered through a series a muscle spasms.

Suddenly the girl approached him, looked up and said, "You shouldn't have killed my daddy."

Dan felt his heart drop into the well of his stomach as he dragged the girl out onto the porch. Red and blue lights flashed across the child's twisted face as a low rumble of words escaped her.

Dan knelt, trying to hear what she was saying, but, through the commotion, her words seemed distant and foreign, her voice seeming cold and adult-like in contrast to her small childlike appearance.

Suddenly wind gusted, blowing tree limbs and shaking leaves into the air. Cool winds sent goosebumps down Dan's forearms as he peered into the night sky in search of dark clouds moving in or lightning flashing in the distance.

He saw only a cloudless expanse filled with stars and a cold dagger of a moon jabbing through the surrounding night.

He looked back into the front yard where a mass of leaves swarmed across the yard sending officers scurrying for shelter.

Dan made his way through the whirlwind, glancing back upon the small child with arms outstretched to the sky, eyes shut tightly.

Her arms suddenly dropped and her eyes flashed open as the wind quickly died. Leaves drifted gracefully to the ground.

Toward the back of the yard, Dan noticed something strange. The big elm tree had been totally stripped of leaves and bark. It now appeared lifeless, its branches gnarled into a hideous, mammoth entity which almost seemed to be frozen, its twisted limbs extended as if to be grasping toward the scene before it.

Dan shivered as he stared in disbelief. Every other tree in

the yard, as well as in neighboring properties, remained mysteriously untouched by the sudden fury.

******

As Patrick Janson made his rounds through the children's shelter, he looked for his daughter, Lindsey, who he had brought to work to play with some of the other children who resided there. Lindsey always made friends and served as therapeutic interaction with others her age by being a link back to the normal world from which they were all separated.

Nancy, his assistant, called from down the hall, "Lindsey's outside with the new girl, Katie."

"Thanks," Patrick said, waving.

He turned and glanced out into the fenced-in yard where the two girls huddled around a tree.

Patrick lifted the window and yelled, "Lindsey, come on. Your mother should be here to pick you up any moment."

Lindsey remained still, unresponsive to his words.

"Lindsey, come on!"

Patrick saw no other movement so he walked to the door and exited.

"Lindsey."

Patrick felt a sense of dread, like there was something wrong with his daughter. His walk suddenly broke into a sprint as he arrived at the base of the tree to see one of his patients, Katie, snickering.

"What's wrong?" he yelled, turning his daughter around to face him.

Patrick shook his daughter softly as she continued to stare on in horror.

"What happened to her?" Patrick asked Katie whose expression suddenly dulled to a serious unblinking stare.

Being a clinical psychologist, he was well-equipped in dealing with this sort of thing with patients, but never his own daughter. His daughter showed signs of shock and trauma, though there was nothing even remotely around that could have caused such a case.

Patrick leaned his back against the tree and ran his fingers through Lindsey's golden-blonde hair. "Munchkin. Hey, Daddy's here. What's the matter?"

Suddenly she blinked then screamed, wrapping her arms around his neck. He picked her up and set his sights on Katie. She smiled and giggled softly. Before he could catch his breath, he had carried Lindsey back into the shelter and into his office where his wife was waiting to pick her up.

******

Patrick worked late that night, reviewing Katie's file. Her father had been recently deceased, her mother had died during her birth. She had been in the custody of the state after her father had been shot during a murder spree in which he had killed six people and wounded a dozen more over a six mile stretch that had ended in the Renshaw Trailer Park on the outskirts of town.

She was assigned to Patrick for mental observations and detection of repressed behavior before she was to be given to foster parents. But since Katie had been there less than three weeks, she had shown no signs of ill-effects from witnessing her father's spree and his death by gunfire from police.

An officer Callahan had contacted Patrick several days ago about discussing certain matters about Katie. He had left another phone message, claiming he would stop by the following morning. Patrick replayed the message, disturbed at how the voice sounded: unstable and shaky, stuttering through the receiver, sounding more like one of his patients than an actual police officer.

He deleted the message as a soft autumn breeze blew through his open window, rattling the Venetian blinds. In the distance, he listened to the dying sounds of insects and frogs. And through all the night sounds, he swore he heard a faint giggle echo from somewhere in the night.

\*\*\*\*\*\*

Later that night, Patrick sat at the edge of his daughter's bed as she drifted closer to sleep. Lindsey had been acting normally since returning home from the shelter. Patrick thought back to the afternoon. Seeing his daughter like that still bothered him as did his failure to pinpoint what may have caused the odd behavior. The fear of his daughter succumbing to seizures or disease swept through his thoughts.

"Daddy," Lindsey said, pulling the sheets around her neck, "Why doesn't Katie have a mommy or a daddy?"

Patrick glanced at his daughter's serious expression. He ran his hand through her hair and smiled.

"They're not around anymore, munchkin."

"You're not going anywhere, are you?"

Patrick shook his head. "No, why?"

Lindsey shrugged. "'Cause Katie said you would be leaving soon."

Patrick tensed, shifted at the edge of the bed. "Is that why you were acting funny earlier?"

"No." His daughter looked away as if she was trying to distance herself.

Patrick sighed in frustration, still wondering why Katie would say something like that. And what did she mean? Patrick suddenly felt helpless, as if his entire life, becoming what his daughter liked to call "a mind doctor," was nothing but a wasted effort, a dead-end maze. Through college and into his profession, he had always felt like he could make a difference. Until today.

"Daddy, I feel sorry for Katie. She's sad and lonely and she's been that way all her life."

"I know. I feel sorry for her too."

"She's so sad, she talks to monsters and they talk back. Sometimes they appear in trees and clouds."

Patrick squinted, taking in his daughter's serious face. Perhaps she was referring to an imaginary game the girls had played or possibly made-up stories Katie had claimed were true. He felt his bewilderment envelope him. Lindsey's pale face flashed back from earlier in the afternoon and Patrick suddenly felt sick to his stomach. He knew he would never let Lindsey visit the shelter again. There was something sinister about Katie and he didn't want it affecting his daughter.

"Go to bed now, darling."

****** 

Officer Callahan was waiting the next morning. Patrick was startled by the tall officer dressed in plain clothes. The man's face was stark white. Dark circles fell around his eyes. His hands shook and his eyes darted around the room.

"Dr. Janson, I wanted to speak with you about Katie."

"Yes, go ahead."

"You haven't placed her yet, have you?"

Patrick sat at his desk and opened his briefcase. "There was a couple in here last week interested in taking her, but I needed more time for observations."

Callahan suddenly peered behind him toward the open door as if he expected someone or something to be looking in. He ran his hand across his face and sighed. "Have you read the papers lately?"

"No," Patrick replied, "I don't often get the chance."

"There's been some weird things going on," Callahan continued, "And I think they have to do with Katie."

Patrick leaned back in his chair, confused. "Go on."

"Since that shootout, strange things have been happening. It started with a tornado-like storm that night, injuring several officers. Nobody's talking, they're all too freaked out about it."

Patrick shifted watching the man as he continually

rubbed his forehead, cheeks and chin. His bloodshot eyes darted around the room, then out the window, and back toward the hallway.

"She's evil, doctor. She caused it all. Hell, I think she even caused her father to flip out and kill those people."

"That's purely speculation," Patrick stated, convinced he had been right about his preconceptions of this man. Obviously too many years on the force, a breakdown from stress, possibly. But there was something that kept gnawing at Patrick's thoughts: Katie's cold stares and the sinister little giggles. Maybe Callahan wasn't crazy after all. Maybe Katie had caused his instability. Sometimes Katie's girlish smiles mutated into a wicked glare or hollow gaze before turning back to the charmed appearance of flushed cheeks, brown eyes and golden locks of hair that curled toward the ends. "What makes you think that?"

"Since that night, all twelve officers on the scene have died, except me. Morgan was found dead, tangled in roots, sucked underground in his own back yard. Carlton died of a massive infection that spread up his arm and leg from that night when he was scratched by a falling limb. Brady was on patrol when his car plunged into a lake. And there's been someone who has been following me the last couple of days. I see him out my window at night, but when I go down to the street, he's gone."

"Have you told your supervisor about this man?"

"No, but just days before they were killed, I heard both Jim and Roman talking about someone following them."

"So what makes you think this is Katie and not the man who has been following you?"

"When I went into the house that night, that girl said that I shouldn't have killed her father. Her face seemed threatening, all twisted and evil-looking. Like she had something already planned for me. And when she stepped outside, strange things began to happen. And even through the wind and everything, I could hear her giggling."

"Well, I'll keep an eye out, " Patrick said, rising from his desk.

"Just don't place her yet, doctor. She's dangerous, she needs to be locked up."

Patrick laughed nervously. "You can't lock up an eight-year-old."

******

Throughout the afternoon, Patrick feared Callahan would return. He had Nancy monitor all the doors, making sure they remained locked between visitors and deliveries.

He paced the hallway, still wondering about his daughter and how she had acted during the previous day. He felt a tremendous sense of dread about Katie staying at the shelter. He knew she wasn't ready to be placed, but he wanted her far away from Lindsey and his family. He wanted to return to that feeling where everything was normal and safe.

These thoughts triggered guilt. Patrick knew Katie had been raised in a dysfunctional family, and that he may have the chance to correct her, but at what price? His daughter's normality? There was an even greater chance that he might not be able to help her since her early years were obviously spent in neglect and abandonment, influenced by a criminal father and haunted by the mystery of her mother's death while giving birth to her.

"There's a couple in your office, doctor." Nancy said, passing him in the hall.

"What do they want?"

"It's the couple from last week who asked about taking Katie."

Patrick breathed deeply. "Where's Katie?"

Nancy led Patrick to the toy room where Katie sat playing. Dolls, teddy bears, and a pink plastic phone surrounded her. She picked up the toy phone and mumbled into the receiver.

"I'll go bring them in," Nancy said, waving at Katie who

waved back. Patrick watched Katie's innocent smile contort to a cold stare after Nancy shut the door. He felt suddenly cold and scared. There was something weird about the room, like it had somehow changed. A cool draught fell upon his body. He felt as if someone else was watching him, or present in the room. He scanned the room, listening through silence, and detected nothing.

Katie held out the phone. "It's for you!"

"Hello," a low-pitched voice suddenly shouted through the receiver, vibrating the plastic. Patrick flinched and shuffled backwards, almost tripping over his own feet. He looked around the room. His heart pounded, his hands shook.

"Oh my God," he whispered as the phone writhed like a snake in Katie's hands.

Through the plastic receiver, a voice echoed. "Pick up the phone, Doctor. Pick it up now!"

Patrick slowly reached for the phone. The cord twisted into a knot then suddenly grew still.

Katie watched and giggled. The wild, hollow look had crept into her glossy eyes once again. The look frightened Patrick. Her eyes seemed much older than she, as if they possessed an old woman's knowledge trapped in her eight-year-old stature.

Patrick grabbed the warm, moist receiver and held it up to his ear. It pulsed and vibrated with a low rumble of laughter.

"Who is this?" Patrick yelled, then the phone suddenly melted in his hand.

"What do they want, Katie?"

Katie forced a giggle. "They wanna play. They ask me things."

"What kind of things?"

"Lots of things. Mostly, they just want me to bring them to life."

"You can bring them to life?"

"Yes," Katie said, smiling. "I think real hard and it

happens."

Patrick shook his head. "This can't be happening!"

The door opened. Nancy and the couple walked in.

For a moment, Patrick wondered if it was all a dream. But the half-twisted smile on Katie's face informed him differently.

The woman, Kathleen, laughed at Katie's face which had changed to an angelic smile, her big brown eyes staring back as she pulled at the braids in her blonde pigtails. "How's she doing, Doctor? We just had to stop by...we both couldn't stop thinking about her all week!"

"I even had dreams about us together as a family," the man named Paul said, putting an arm around his wife and pulling her close. He leaned towards Patrick and whispered, "Is she ready for us yet?"

Patrick stared down at the phone as Katie wrapped herself around his leg, the animal-like glare in her eyes sending shockwaves of fear rippling throughout his body.

"You're in luck," Patrick stated, "I think she's ready to be placed."

******

An hour after Katie and her new family had departed, Patrick sat silently, slouching in his office.

"I forgot to pick up Katie's drawings," Nancy said, standing in the front doorway. "Can you gather them up with her crayons and finger paint? Paul and Kathleen are going to pick them up first thing tomorrow."

"Drawings?"

"Yes," Nancy replied. "She's been coloring a lot lately."

"I'll get them."

"And don't forget to lock up," Nancy yelled as she closed the door and disappeared into the parking lot.

Patrick switched on the bedroom light and picked up the box full of papers beside Katie's old bed. He glanced at the stack of colored pictures and a strange drawing suddenly disturbed him. On the top page, a figure, which resembled Patrick in the same suit, was drawn being strangled by a pink telephone.

Patrick stared down in disbelief. Quickly he flipped to the next page where a tall, dark slender figure stood, tapering to a point, like a wisp of smoke.

Patrick turned over more pages until he came to a collage painting of two stick figure-humans and a dog with a knife sticking in. Red tears dripped from their empty eye sockets. It was labeled: "MY NEW FAMILY."

Sweat trickled down Patrick's cheek as he looked on. His heart thumped, swelling with blood.

He turned to the next page only to notice that the center had been cut out in the form of a jagged, pointed knife. He noticed the paper shavings scattered on the floor around him. He knelt and picked up a scrap piece when the paper gouged his index finger, sticking in his flesh. A bead of blood formed at the tip as Patrick realized the paper shavings had hardened and turned sharp and smooth like metal.

Patrick dropped the papers onto the floor. The room spun around him as he saw the final page slip from the bottom of the stack, drift in front of him and land face up.

Patrick glanced onto the page and his breath was taken.

"No!" he screamed. Please, no!"

The final page was a detailed drawing labeled "MY NEW PLAYMATE" with a small girl playing on a swing at dusk. She swung from a tree that was changing into something alive, something watching and waiting as tentacle-limbs weaved their way into the rope which supported the wooden swing.

The familiar lines in the little girl's face jumped out at Patrick as the entire drawing seemed to come to life right in front of his eyes. Sickened by the image, he remembered how his daughter always waited in the backyard for him to return from work.

The sketch slowly came to life, each crayon line swelling and contracting into motion. The swing moved, the ropes frayed as claws now gripped the child's bottom, swinging her faster toward the trunk of the tree where a deep, dark notch existed revealing an open orifice.

In the distance, braided pigtails stuck out from behind a row of shrubs as small hands stretched outward, summoning the monstrous thing to escape its captive reality, breathe and exist.

"No, Lindsey!" Patrick cried, watching his daughter swing across the face of the wrinkled piece of paper.

Patrick reached into his pocket for the cell phone. He quickly dialed his home number to the voice of his wife.

"Where's Lindsey?" he yelled. "Where is she?"

"Calm down, Patrick," his wife said. "Katie rode her bike over here. I couldn't believe her new family let her, but she said that she wanted to play with Lindsey. Wasn't that sweet?"

"Where are they?"

"Calm down. There just in the back yard swinging."

Patrick dropped the receiver.

"This can't be real..it can't be happening," he screamed and searched the floor for the first drawing. After finding it, he positioned the papers in front of him. The paper labeled "MY NEW FAMILY" suddenly caught his attention. The knife, once in the dog, was now rising off the page and plunging its way into the male and female stick figures.

The dog squirmed across the page, already mortally wounded from the incisions across its throat and abdomen. Blood accumulated on the paper below its mouth. The paper folded and crumpled between Patrick's hands from the movement of the knife sinking into the bodies and the dog crawling across its surface.

Patrick glanced back upon the picture with his daughter swinging. The swing was now empty, the tree no longer alive. But in the dark notch, he saw the only remaining movement: a leg flailing from inside the small hole.

Without another thought, Patrick grabbed his car keys and ran for the door.

He stopped in the middle of the shelter, noticing a dark figure blocking the door. Suddenly he remembered the drawing with the strange, slender person.

This figure, now standing before him, waved a long bony finger at him. Its body moved through the air like a thundercloud eclipsing clear skies. Its face was scarred and eroded by a single bullet hole.

Beyond the doorway lay what remained of Officer Callahan. A blood-smeared path trailed from his body, stretching down the walkway and into the road.

"My Katie," the dark figure whispered, "What have you done with my child?"

The stench of grave dirt and formaldehyde wafted through the room.

Patrick collapsed in a quivering heap upon the floor, helplessly sobbing as he listened to footsteps staggering closer.

Taking in the intruder's reeking stench, Patrick suddenly remembered his daughter's words, *Katie said you would be leaving too.*

Patrick tensed, feeling cold, clammy hands gripping his neck. Down the hallway, he watched as the pink telephone turned the corner and began inching its way toward him.

# ROAD KILL

T he country road twisted through fields of corn and wheat, past old picturesque farmhouses and barns lodged between rolling hills decorated with cattle. Alone on the small highway, Clay drove his Ford Taurus, basking in the afternoon sun.

Clay watched the pavement wavering with what seemed to be steam rising from its surface. Muddy tracks of farm machinery eclipsed the double yellow lines. And ahead, something lay in the road.

From a distance, Clay saw it was a dead animal, its body contorted in impossible angles, mashed and crushed into the black asphalt.

Clay squinted at the thing, trying to decipher what kind of animal it was. It looked like a raccoon, but the color was hard to make out. Fluids coated its body, painting the center of the road in crimson.

As Clay drove closer, he thought it might be a possum, though the pink fleshy tail was missing. He remembered seeing the damn things running across the roadway, seeing headlights, then running down the roadway along with his car until the tires struck. The dumb creatures littered the roadside in what seemed to be the thousands.

But there was something different about this animal. It was like a skunk or a full-grown farm cat in size, but without any recognizable features.

Clay smiled as his car approached the mess. He steered the car away from the splotch, then suddenly veered back, hitting the thing. The car shook slightly, tires snapping cartilage and bone. The thing tumbled forward as Clay watched from his rearview mirror as it rolled into the ditch.

Clay laughed.

Suddenly, out of the ditch the thing crawled, hobbling up the roadway.

Clay stopped the car, turned his head and watched it drawing closer.

"Good God," he said to himself. "What in the hell is it?"

The road kill picked up speed, its legs flailing from side to side, dragging behind it portions of its insides dropping onto the roadside.

Clay could vaguely make out its face beneath the matted, blood-stained fur. Its bulging eyes were alert and focused on Clay. The sound of its skin dragging against asphalt sent a sick chill down his back.

The car sputtered, then died.

*Christ, this is like a bad horror story*, Clay thought. He turned the key, firing the ignition, then wiped the sweat from his forehead and drove away.

The thing disappeared as he sped off.

Clay looked back and chuckled, "Maybe it can catch a ride with the next Amish buggy."

Lights flashed ahead. Gates descended as a train made its way through the crossing.

"Oh Jesus," he whispered, keeping an eye on his rearview mirror. "Come on!"

He pulled up to the crossing and waited.

Down the road, the thing came. It was only a speck but getting bigger, rapidly advancing, jerking its body from side to side, pulling its innards along behind it.

The train slowed.

The car died.

Clay screamed, "This can't be happening! Start dammit!"

He turned the key. The engine gurgled. Nothing.

He turned the key again, pumping the accelerator. Nothing.

Clay slammed his fists against the steering wheel, looked back down the road. Nothing. The road kill was gone.

Clay laughed, shaking his head. What was he afraid of anyway?

The train passed. The gates lifted.

Clay turned the key again, the car started, and he drove over the tracks.

Claws suddenly scraped against the roof.

Quickly Clay rolled up his window as he accelerated.

The thing slid down the windshield. A trail of blood smeared across the glass, blocking his view. Maggots wriggled amongst the carnage.

Clay flipped on his wipers, but it only smeared the mess more. He pressed for the wiper fluid, but nothing came out.

Gravel flew against the side of the car.

He pulled the car back into the roadway. Driving madly, he turned the wipers on high speed as he swerved trying to knock the thing from his hood.

Slowly the wipers cleared the blood to the sight of the combine with a yellow and orange striped, triangular sign on the back.

Clay screamed.

\*\*\*\*\*\*

Broken glass surrounded him on the hot burning pavement. The stench of manure and death hung in the air.

Looking for his car, Clay lifted his head enough to notice his legs buckled behind his back, his index finger a few feet from his arm, and something furry crawling onto his face.

Clay vomited beneath the thing as the smell seemed to add to his paralysis.

"Help," he yelled, but the sound was muffled beneath the half-rotted carcass which squirmed atop him.

## I'LL BE DAMNED | 62

*Please, farmer, don't be dead. Save me from this...thing.*
Then a sound erupted down the road. Tires spinning on asphalt.

*Yes! Help.*

The thing on his face slowly spread itself over his chest, dripping organ fragments and juices down into his torn shirt. Clay cringed as the sticky heat of its body stretched down his stomach, past his legs finally covering his shattered kneecaps.

Clay managed to raise his hand, attempting to push the thing off him, but its skin stretched, vomiting a mass of intestines into his face.

The sound of a vehicle grew closer.

\*\*\*\*\*\*

"Yuck! What's that, honey?"

The bearded man driving a car squinted. "Some poor animal."

A voice from the back seat said, "Look daddy, it's still moving."

"Kids, turn your heads. I'm going to have to put the poor thing out of its misery."

The woman in the passenger side covered the children's eyes and motioned toward the combine alongside the road. "Just watch out for that farm machinery."

"Okay dear."

The man swerved.

The car veered slightly.

Bones crunched beneath the wheels.

# THE SPECIAL DISH

Yin Su scrubbed the stranger's table for the third time as the slender man stared, tapping his fingers against the plate. Out of the corner of his eye, Yin Su saw his manager motioning for him.

"How about this. Good?"

The man shook his head. "It will have to do. At least now I won't have to feel for my fork under three inches of dust!"

Yin Su bowed, then returned to where his manager stood, noticeably perspiring under his suit jacket. The manager grabbed Yin Su by the arm and whispered, "A friend from the paper just called to inform me that Bruce Lebowitz, the food critic for the *Sun Times,* is here and he's reviewing our restaurant for tomorrow's edition. That's him!"

Yin Su took in a deep breath and glanced at the slender man browsing the menu. "Ah, man in paper."

"Yes, please don't fuck this one up or we're finished. My friend tells me this guy's a real asshole, so just deal with him and make him happy."

Yin Su shook his head and returned to the man's table.

"Sir, ready to order?"

The food critic looked up and half-smiled. "A real Chinaman working here. Real nice touch. Most of these shitholes are run by a bunch of lousy Americans who couldn't even nuke a hotdog."

Yin Su smiled and bowed. "Not here. At Golden China Palace, we have real thing."

"The real shit, huh. We'll see about that."

"Are you ready, sir."

The food critic rolled his eyes. "First of all, tell me...is it true that all you Chinese guys have little dorks?"

Yin Su shrugged his shoulders. "Dorks?"

The food critic sipped his wine and swallowed. "Yeah, you know Cocks...little cocks. Do all you Chinamen have small wangs, minuscule peckers, microscopic love muscles?"

Yin Su took another deep breath. "You're ready to order then?"

The food critic glared at Yin Su, shook his head, and rolled his eyes. "Suppose I need a fucking interpreter just to order."

Yin Su gripped the pen tighter, trying to mask his anger.

"Okay Chinaman, listen closely: Chick-en-Lo-Mein-with-Fried-Rice-and-Egg-Drop-Soup. And please clean this awful silverware. Looks like somebody just shoved it up their ass!"

Yin Su grabbed the silverware, and returned to the kitchen. He slammed the utensils into the sink. "Stupid-ass, sonofbitch!"

The manager entered, responding to the noise. "Settle down. You have an attitude like that and that asshole's going to shut this place down. The whole town reads his fucking column."

"Yes sir, sorry sir." Yin Su replied.

Fifteen minutes later the cook placed the dish on the counter and Yin Su inspected its contents. The noodles and chicken were well-cooked and vegetables and sauce steaming. He noticed how decorative the plate looked. Yin Su wiped down another set of silverware until it was spotless and proceeded to deliver the food critic's meal.

"Enjoy," Yin Su said, smiling. "You like anything else?"

The food critic returned a dark glare. "How about some privacy?"

Yin Su bowed and turned.

SHANE RYAN STALEY / 65

Suddenly silverware crashed against a plate.

"Hey Chinaman, am I suppose to eat this chicken or dribble it down a basketball court," the food critic shouted. "I'm not eating this shit. I've seen enough of this place!"

Suddenly the manager cut in.

"Is there something wrong, sir?"

The food critic picked up a piece of chicken and flung it at Yin Su, smacking him on the face. Yin Su flinched, took two steps toward the man and stopped. He knew he needed to keep his job. It was his only source of income until he could better adapt himself to the American language and way of life.

"Yes there's something wrong. Ying Wang Dingitty Dang over there just served me a cold, rubbery dish of God-knows-what and it just so happens that I'm reviewing this joke-of-a-restaurant in tomorrow's paper. So I suggest you find yourself another profession because I'm personally taking this place down!"

"I'm very sorry, sir," the manager said. "Please accept my apology—"

Yin Su grabbed the food critic's arm and guided him back down into his seat. "No, I am sorry, sir. I will see to it you get a special dish on house. I make it myself."

The food critic glanced at the manager, then back to Yin Su. "Are you serious?"

Yin Su nodded. He looked over at his stuttering boss and nodded, giving him a look of seriousness. "A special dish I learned to make in China."

The food critic laughed. "This I got to see. And I'll tell you what. If I like it, I'll let you off the hook, but if I don't — I'm going to make this place the laughing stock of the town. You'll be lucky if the bums will even eat out of your trash dumpsters!"

Yin Su returned to the kitchen, rolling up his sleeves.

The manager stormed through the door, following closely behind. "What in the hell do you think you're doing. You're not the cook!"

"From where I come from, everyone is cook."

Yin Su cut pieces of meat and vegetables, sprinkled herbs and sauces, and stirred the collage together. He glanced at the manager who stared on in amazement. Yin Su, after cooking the dish, pulled out a strange bottle filled with a thick red liquid.

"What's that?" the manager inquired.

Yin Su smiled and shook the bottle as it foamed vigorously, spilling over the sides of the partially-capped top. "Secret ingredient. Old family recipe."

The manager followed him to the food critic's table as he served him. Yin Su smiled and puffed out his chest as the critic took his first bite.

The food critic swallowed the first heaping spoonful and puckered his face. He turned toward Yin Su and cursed. "That is disgusting, you sonofabitch! Golden China Palace is history!"

Yin Su watched as the slender man put both hands on his stomach as he almost doubled over before exiting.

Yin Su's laugh was cut short by the manager's red face. "What the hell were you trying to prove?"

Yin Su took off his apron, handed it to the manager and said, "You have nothing to worry about."

The manager grabbed Yin Su by the collar and shoved his index finger into his face. "I'm bringing the paper in the morning. If that asshole gives us a bad review, it's your job!"

Yin Su smiled. "I will be here first thing tomorrow to open up."

****** 

Bruce Lebowitz, the food critic, stumbled outside, feeling his stomach churn and burn. A pain shot through his midsection

"God damn rotten Chink. He's going to wish he never fucked with me. Special dish, my ass."

The pain grew worse, his stomach cramped. Sweat

beaded on his forehead as cold chills coursed through his entire body.

Bruce stopped to lean against a building. People walked by, staring as he spread his legs. A stabbing pressure shot through his bowels.

A small boy tugged on his trench coat. "Hey mister, you all right?"

Holding his stomach, he carefully released the pressure. A burning stream of air slowly squeezed its way through his butt cheeks. His anus burned.

"Get away from me kid."

The pressure subsided as he stood and took in a deep breath.

A strange, noxious smell rose from the depths of his pants, slowly drifting in sour pockets which burned his nose.

He fanned his face, trying to push the odor away, but it clung to him.

He walked away, cutting down an alleyway, but every breath he took filled his lungs with the pungent, rotted stench.

He felt his chest heaving for fresh air, but the warm, odorous scent hung like a cloud circling his head.

He felt a pain in his chest. A shortness of breath. He stumbled out into the street, grabbing a woman by the arm. His face was burning.

The woman fanned her face, covered her nose. "Get away from me, creep!"

A man pointed at him. "Look, his face...it's blue. And God, he sure stinks."

"Maybe he's hyperventilating."

Someone suddenly rushed to his aid, holding a brown paper sack over his nose and mouth. Bruce whirled around, seeing the man's watery eyes squinting. The man held the sack tighter around Bruce's face. He inhaled, smelling the foul odor trapped in the paper bag.

He wretched and vomited into the paper bag. He heaved again, sending another stream which popped the bag, splattering the man's face. A piece of partially-digested chicken bounced across the sidewalk.

Bruce grabbed his throat, fighting for a breath away from the overwhelming stench.

He took in a final breath of his own flatulence as everything blurred.

\*\*\*\*\*\*

At the hospital, his lifeless body was inspected. The doctor called in another doctor who, in turn, called for another doctor. After hearing eyewitness testimony, they were perplexed as to how a man in the middle of a downtown sidewalk could die of carbon dioxide poisoning.

\*\*\*\*\*\*

Yin Su swept the floor as the manager entered, slapping the paper in front of his face.

"You poisoned him, didn't you?"

Yin Su shook his head. "I did no such thing."

"Then why in place of his review column, is there his obituary?"

Yin Su continued sweeping as a smile washed over his face. "Paper should read '*Man killed by own fart*.'"

The manager's jaw dropped. "I thought I told you never to make that dish again. That's why I fired you as a cook."

"It wasn't same dish as last time."

"Well last time I had to pay the hospital bill to put some poor gentleman's intestines back on the correct side of his asshole," the manager said, shaking his head. "The doctors said it looked like he had blown a party favor out his ass!"

Yin Su chuckled and patted his boss on the back. "This time I got it right."

SHANE RYAN STALEY / 69

# POINT OF INTEREST

It would go down as the most hellish vacation in family history.

James always hated family outings, especially cross-country ones. His father had mapped out the entire Midwest with red dots from Ohio to Illinois, on through Indiana and Kentucky — like some kind of twisted connect-the-dot voyage — as a lame way of spending family time together.

James adjusted his Megadeth concert tee-shirt, brushed his black-dyed hair from his eyes and focused on his geeky sister staring out the car window and pointing at things that held little interest to James. His father bobbed back and forth in the driver's seat, whistling some queer sing-along which nobody dared to join in. His mother just sat in the passenger's seat, wide-eyed and smiling with buck-teeth and black-rimmed glasses straight from the sixties.

*This is a fucking nightmare,* James thought. Each time they drove next to a public setting, James crouched out of view so no one could see a sixteen-year-old boy subjected to such an embarrassing scenario.

His father's whistling suddenly stopped and the car slowed. His father pointed to a square green sign which read: POINT OF INTEREST 1 Mile.

"Let's check this out, it must be something neat," his father said.

"But this isn't on the fucking map," James replied.

His mother's head turned, eyebrows arched. "Watch your language, mister!"

The car slowed off the roadway to a clearing. James looked ahead, seeing a stone structure jutting out of the ground. A dense cluster of trees and dark overgrowth spread behind the structure as far as he could see.

His father darted from the car followed by his sister and mother.

"Fuck!" James said, then reluctantly opened the door. After riding for three hours straight and holding his piss in for almost two, James figured he could sneak off, stretch a little and drain it before they were finished.

"Come here, James," his father yelled. "Check out this neat-looking well."

James rolled his eyes, his fists clinched up. "Hopefully it's a wishing well and I can wish this whole fucking trip away," James whispered to himself.

James strolled up to the rock foundation and peered into the darkness. The circular stone walls of the well delved deeply to where even the mid-afternoon sunlight couldn't reach. His mother pulled a flashlight out of her purse and aimed it into the well. The beam dissolved into layers of darkness.

"Wowwee, that's some deep well," he father said. "Neat-o, huh kids?"

"There's usually some kind of sign telling why this spot is so significant," his father said, glancing around the area. James looked around as well, but found no such sign.

His father took the flashlight and waved it around in the darkness. "Probably a natural spring or possibly the world's deepest well."

James looked into the wooded area, searching for a thick set of trees before he became a natural spring himself. As he glanced back into the well, something caught his attention. His father had stopped moving the flashlight and was concentrating on one particular side. He glanced over at his father whose wide glossy eyes remained unblinking.

"Dad," James said. "Hey, Dad."

James looked back into the well and saw a face in the beam of light. And then a hand rose from the darkness, a voice calling for his father.

"Walt, they're going to air-raid this place," the man yelled up at his father.

His sister gasped in horror while his mother screamed "Oh my God, Walter, there's a man down there who knows your name!"

James squinted at the man who seemed to be crawling up the wall toward them. He was wearing army fatigues, his hands and face bloody.

Beads of sweat trickled down his father's face as he stared on in utter disbelief. His father had served in Vietnam for two years, an experience he seldom talked about. His service there had changed him so much, caused his mental breakdown and personality change which transformed him from a high school star football player to an almost helpless, sometimes infantile, middle-aged geek without any clue toward social acceptance.

His father's look of horror changed quickly to sadness. "Billy-Joe, is that really you? I thought you were dead."

The soldier in the well clawed at the wall. "Help me, Walt, they're going to raid this place. You have to help me out this time. Don't leave me here like you did in Nam."

His father broke into tears. "I'm so sorry, Billy-Joe. God, I'm so sorry for leaving you there to die. But it was either you or the both of us, so I had to save my own life."

The man slipped into darkness, then emerged again smearing blood over the murky wall. "They're down here, Walt, help me fight them off. Be a man this time — make up for the past."

James watched his father shake and weep louder, covering his face.

"Honey, let's get out of here." His mother put a hand on his father's shoulder.

"Help me, Walt. Don't let me down this time."

His father's gaze at the wounded soldier intensified. His lip quivered uncontrollably.

Suddenly his father ripped off his sport coat and bow tie and handed James his glasses and flashlight. A look of determination filled his father's face as he lunged toward the well and grabbed the soldier's arm.

The soldier disintegrated and his father fell forward into darkness.

James watched his mother scream and run toward the edge of the well. "Oh my God, Walter. Walter! Are you okay?"

James listened for splashing water or just a violent splat, but heard nothing.

As his mother leaned into the well yelling, James flashed the beam on a slow movement creeping up the wall. At first he thought it was a giant snail, but as it came closer he saw the gelatinous bloodied body, small and distorted half-formed limbs pulling itself along the wall. Its beady black eyes stared up at his mother.

"Mommy, hold me."

His mother's eye widened in shock.

"Mommy, nurse me," it said.

A mix of fear and love crossed his mother's face and James suddenly knew what it was. It was baby Steven, the first child conceived but miscarried in his mother's third month. James remembered hearing hushed stories told on cold nights about the terrible night when his would've-been brother ceased to be nurtured any longer inside its womb. Flashes of an image of a bloody mass fallen into the toilet and his mother's frantic calls to the doctor circled in his head from the few stories that were ever told.

"Help me, Mommy," it gurgled.

His mother leaned into the well trying to grab it, but couldn't reach. James heard his sister yelling for her to stop, but his mother ignored her and stretched farther, but to no avail.

"Oh my poor precious baby. I'm so sorry Mommy couldn't have taken better care of you while you were inside me."

James couldn't help but to stare down at the blob of twisted bones and fleshy nubs and bloody sinew.

His mother broke down into tears. She leaned over the edge, letting herself fall toward her half-formed child.

And again James listened for impact, but no sounds came except for a little gurgle, perhaps a giggle, which emanated from the thing before it disappeared.

His sister was overcome with panic. She circled the well, crying while looking at James. James stood there staring into darkness, still listening for his parents to hit bottom.

After staring into nothingness for what seemed eternity, James was suddenly distracted by his sister's voice.

"You're such a cute horsie."

James looked up to see his sister staring into the well. When James refocused into the darkness, he saw a flash of bright white. A little unicorn had galloped up the wall, settling to gaze up at his sister.

"Jeanie, that ain't no fucking horse!" James said. But his sister was already straddling the edge with her arm extended, ready to stroke the animal.

She quickly fell forward into nothingness.

Minutes passed and James still listened, but heard nothing that even resembled impact. The only sound he heard were three echoes that sounded more like deep guttural belches than anything.

The pressure in his balls suddenly crept back to his attention as he parted the weeds, unzipped his fly, and drained himself. As he shook himself dry, he peered up at a sign tangled in vines, hidden from the roadway. He tore the vines away to the site description: GATEWAY TO HELL.

"Cool," he muttered, peering around the dense weeds and twisted trees to where the cold stone foundation loomed.

Quickly he zipped his fly, rushed toward the well, and hopped in.

## I'LL BE DAMNED | 74

# THE DEAD SANTA

T ears welled in Santa's eyes as he stared across the snowy windswept field. Blood seeped into the snow as elves and reindeer lay shot to death, bodies jerking slower as the North Pole's arctic air gusted, freezing flesh and bone.

Santa dropped the gun and cupped his hands over his face. He couldn't believe what he had done. The countless lists from children had been pouring in at a fevered pace. Stress levels were high. Santa, being burned out at making toys year 'round, sought his escape by sneaking into his den to watch pornos. Santa knew he had become obsessed with these videos. He no longer cared about anything else, including his job. He found himself spiraling out of control, growing more hostile toward Mrs. Claus and the elves, but he never thought it would have progressed to this.

Santa heard a muffled cry as he looked up to see Lorel, his favorite elf, still alive, but convulsing wildly in a snow drift. Santa lifted the gun to the elf's head and pulled the trigger. Brain matter sprayed across the snow until it resembled oatmeal floating across a sea of milk.

Mrs. Claus would be home soon. Santa was petrified that he would lose her after she took one glance at what he had done. Where would he go? What would he do? He knew he could no longer continue to deliver gifts on Christmas because his heart now belonged to porn, not to the children.

Santa fell to his knees and cried. He lifted the gun, jamming the barrel into his mouth. His finger shook against the trigger.

A strange sight suddenly distracted him. A mirror image of himself stood next to him, gawking down. But this man's beard had been shaved into a goatee and he sported a black and white suit instead of the traditional red.

"Who are you?" Santa managed to speak, gagging on the barrel.

The man's guttural laugh echoed across the snowy plain. "I think it would be cliché to call me Satan Claus, but you may refer to me as your replacement since your services are about to be terminated." The man's eyes twinkled with mischief.

"What makes you so sure I'll let you take over?" Santa asked, looking back at the man to find that he had changed into a women who wiggled a pair of oversized breasts in his direction. He closed his eyes, but could only conjure other images of blondes and brunettes and red-haired "Santa's Helpers," dressed in leather with whips and chains and candy canes lining up to tease him, please him, and dominate him like all naughty girls wanted to do.

Santa tried to fight the temptation, but could only manage to imagine himself having wild sex with women in the back of his sleigh.

"I'm so sick," he cried, "I don't deserve to be Santa anymore."

He reached out for the woman's breasts and recoiled, shaking his head. "I've got to control myself." He felt the heat of his erection melting away the snow beneath him.

The woman slipped out of her clothes and lay before him, waiting. He shoved the gun deeper into his mouth and pulled the trigger. A brief vision flashed through his mind as the woman melted into the same figure in the black and white suit. Then everything gushed away.

\*\*\*\*\*\*

The stranger smiled as the last gurgling breaths escaped Santa. He looked across the field, taking in the variety of corpses strung atop the snow. With a wave of his hands, the corpses came back from the dead. Elves rose blankly and retreated into the warmth of the toy factory. Reindeer stood, shaking off blood, and huddled once again as a pack.

"This will be a Christmas unlike any other," the dark Santa muttered, hearing sleigh bells echoing across the field. Mrs. Claus drifted closer and the dark Santa snapped his fingers and said, "Take care of her," and the reindeer sprung to life, chasing after her sleigh.

From a distance he watched as the reindeer stomped Mrs. Claus into the snow. The pack settled over her body, picking at her flesh and ripping her limbs apart.

******

Eight-year-old Chris tossed and turned. Christmas morning was only hours away. The neighboring house's lights flashed into his darkened bedroom as he glanced at the clock which read 6:32. He shifted uncomfortably and thought about all the presents he might get. He imagined a big red bicycle with a red bow next to the tree.

Snowflakes drifted outside as he focused on the neighbor's snow-covered roof, wondering how Santa could manage to drag an entire bike down a chimney.

His eyes grew heavy as he watched the hypnotizing flurry of snow fall.

Suddenly he heard bells outside. He jerked upright in bed then wandered groggily over to the window and parted the curtains.

"Santa!" he said.

A rusted sleigh swept down from the sky and skidded across his front lawn, uprooting dead grass and mud. As

Chris looked closer, he noticed the reindeer looked sick and deranged, their bodies missing portions of flesh. Bones protruded from their ribcages, their jaws half-missing.

Chris tried to shake the remnants of dream from his consciousness, but again looked onto the strange site of Santa wearing a black suit. Though he was indeed plump with a big round belly, he was missing a beard — only a spiky white goatee appeared, covered with frost.

Santa spit a large yellowish-green wad of phlegm onto the front lawn then cleared each nostril out. It wasn't long until he located the Bethlehem scene set up next to the mailbox. The dark Santa peered down at the baby Jesus in the manger, then proceeded to punt the tiny plastic figurine across the lawn. It bounced against the siding and settled in the snow-covered bushes.

Chris ran down the hall and opened his parent's bedroom door.

"Mom..Dad..Santa's really here!"

His parents shifted, moaning, half-asleep. "Go back to bed, Chris, it's not morning yet."

"But—"

His father bolted upright at the sound of the front door being kicked in.

"Chris — go to your room and lock the door," his father said, jumping out of bed and grabbing a baseball bat in the closet.

"But it's just Santa!" Chris argued, departing the room for the stairwell.

Halfway down the stairs, the door splintered into fragments as the dark Santa entered.

His father, rushing behind him, tripped on the steps and plummeted down the flight of stairs, landing unconscious beside Chris' feet.

Chris looked up at the Santa, confused. The dark Santa browsed through the house until he found the plate of cookies and milk.

He flung the cookies to the side and dumped the milk into

a plant. "Give you a hint, kid," the strange Santa said, "Next year try liquor and beer nuts — you'll get more presents!"

Chris looked back at his father who was slowly waking up.

"So what do you want for Christmas, kid?"

Chris smiled, feeling excitement pulse through his body. "A big red bicycle."

The dark Santa squinted into the bag and shook his head. "Now how the hell am I suppose to cram a fucking bicycle in here?"

Chris shrugged.

"Fuck the bicycle, kid. Everyone knows bicycles are for queers."

"But how am I suppose to get to my friend Timmy's?"

"Hitchhike or something, I don't give a rat's ass."

The dark Santa rummaged through his burlap bag and pulled forth a pair of women's panties. "Whoops, that's from the last house," he said, his face blushing. He sifted through the bag again and pulled out a Bic lighter. He handed it to Chris with a pack of cigarettes.

"Is this all I get?"

"Yes, you greedy little bastard. Those cigarettes cost an arm and a leg these days."

Chris pouted, crossing his arms.

The dark Santa sighed. "Oh, all right," he said, pulling from his bag a magazine. He tossed it to Chris who scanned the cover and smiled after noticing two young blondes, wrapping their naked bodies around each other, tongues extended into whipcream-filled navels and cleavage.

"Wow!" Chris said, "This is the best present I ever got."

His father grabbed the magazine away and stood before the dark Santa. "You get the hell out of my house or I'm going to beat you senseless, you sonofabitch!"

The dark Santa snapped his fingers as a flash of green and red shot through Chris' vision and knocked his father into an adjacent room. Chris whirled to see a tiny elf lodged onto his father's jugular. Another elf came streaking out of the bathroom, its pale face appearing twisted and deranged.

Chris cringed as the other elf dove toward his father, latching onto his crotch. His father screamed, kicking desperately. The window shattered as more elves jumped atop his father, all biting and burrowing into his father's body.

"Was there anything else on your list, kid?"

Chris managed to pry his attention away from his father's piercing squeals to refocus on the Santa who scratched at his ass and thumbed his nose.

Chris let his eyes fall to the carpet as he shook his head.

The Santa approached him, putting a gloved hand on his shoulder. "Come on, let ol' Santa know what it is."

Chris lifted his head to the deep green eyes of the Santa. "I told the Santa in the mall that I wanted a sister."

His mother suddenly yelled from upstairs. "Richard, what's happening? What was all that noise? I tried to call 911, but the line is dead!"

Santa's eyes flashed with surprise and excitement. "Let me go talk to your mom about getting you a sister."

Chris nodded, flipping open his magazine as the dark Santa ascended the stairs. Once upstairs, he loosened his belt as his black velvety pants dropped around his ankles. Chris peered at his bone-white ass, noticing the Santa smiling as he watched his erection finally appear from beneath his oversized belly.

The elves had finished feasting on his father as most crawled through a broken window and mounted the sleigh. A few others cornered the cat, one holding it down as the other doused it with gasoline. The cat scampered from their grasp as one elf lit a match and the other yelled, "Here kitty, kitty, kitty!"

Minutes of banging and screaming upstairs persisted as Chris waited. A few times he swore he heard his mother yell: "Oh yes, give it to me St. Dick, I've been a very, very naughty girl!" The sound of a belt slapping bare skin echoed through the house.

Finally the dark Santa, along with his mother, appeared

from the bedroom, both with cigarettes dangling from their mouths.

"Hey kid, I think we came to terms on that sister request. You might have to wait a little while though. Probably until the end of October."

Suddenly a cat hissed and screamed as a ball of flame scurried through the living room, smacking against the wall.

The base of the wall caught fire as his mother screamed.

Chris turned to see the dark Santa on his knees, his head disappearing up his mother's bathrobe.

"Mom — the house is burning. Help!"

His mother moaned as the flames rose higher. Chris approached the Santa and kicked him in the ass. The Santa kicked backwards, knocking Chris over.

"Get away from my mother!" he yelled. "You're not really St. Nick — You're St. Prick, you asshole. You're burning my house down! And you've killed my father too!" Chris continued as the realization finally settled that his father was nothing more than bone and gristle on the living room floor.

Chris felt the tears forming in his eyes. He shook his head and curled himself into a ball, rocking back and forth.

He wondered if he had suddenly grown out of his childhood, or that he was just finally old enough to realize that Christmas was just another day filled with horrible events like the ones he had come face to face with on this particular night. Then he wondered if he was trapped in some insane nightmare, and that he might awake to the smell of breakfast and the sight of presents scattered around the tree.

Because this wasn't the way he remembered Christmas from past years. Santa was usually kind and was never seen entering the house. He always ate the cookies and never had sex with his mother after having killed his father.

So far this Christmas was the absolute worst.

Suddenly he heard bells in the sky. He peered out the window and noticed a sleigh with an assortment of healthy-looking reindeer appearing this time along with a white-bearded man adorned in red and white. Chris ran to the window and yelled, "Santa, please help us!"

The sleigh veered and descended, landing on top of the house. Santa slid down the chimney and came out with a fire extinguisher which he sprayed onto the fire until it was no more.

Chris wrapped his arms around the real Santa and sighed in relief. He smelled a strange scent of rot as he looked up into Santa's pale face. This Santa seemed to be missing a portion of his head as grey matter swelled outward from his shattered skull. His eyes were huge, only the whites showed.

The dark Santa rose, wiped off his mouth, and stared at the real Santa who extracted a candy cane which he unwrapped and gnawed one end to a sharp point. They circled, eying one another.

"I thought you were dead," the dark Santa said.

"I am dead," the real Santa returned, holding the candy cane-dagger in front of him, "I'm a zombie now, idiot."

"Kick his ass, Zombie-Santa!" Chris cheered, "Save Christmas for everyone!"

The real Santa, now a zombie, ran a hand over his beard as a finger broke off and fell to the floor. He kicked it aside and focused on the enemy before him.

"Did you think you could take over Christmas so easily?" the real Santa asked.

"Yes," the dark Santa answered, lighting another cigarette. He reached into the bag once again and pulled something out.

The real Santa watched as a blow-up doll emerged. He stared watching the plastic doll inflate to life-size, pockets of air forming around her breasts and midsection. Santa focused on the curvy features until he approached and jumped atop the doll, burying his head into her cleavage.

The doll exploded as the candy cane punctured plastic. A surge of air blew Santa back into the fireplace.

The elves rushed in once again and doused his red suit with gasoline. The dark Santa threw in a starter log and flicked his cigarette on top. Flames quickly engulfed Santa's body, his suit and cap smoldering into instant embers.

As the scent of human flesh wafted through the house, the ghoulish reindeer finished their feast on the living reindeer and rejoined the dark Santa on his sleigh. They took off into the sky, passing the North Star which flickered to black.

On the ground a clan of Christmas carolers approached the house as his mother screamed after noticing what had become of her husband. As the carolers stopped on the porch, Chris noticed that they were all pale and bloated, their faces freshly scarred as they bled onto the steps.

"I'm dreaming of a black Christmas," they sang in unison, "With every goat head that I bite..."

Others chanted from farther down the street, "Silent Night, Eternal Night, All is black, all is right..."

The two groups merged, beating on the door. Sunken faces peered in through windows. Hands reached through broken glass. Icy winds gusted to a chorus of low wails.

Chris took in the whole scene and sighed in disgust. His mother sat rocking back and forth in a dark corner, her complexion appearing paler each passing minute. He envisioned the red bicycle beside the melted plastic tree, then everything in his immediate surroundings faded as a cold gust of wind blew through the cracked windows, stripping the stockings from the mantle.

There were no presents beneath the tree, no joyful Christmas songs playing from the radio. The sun had yet to rise though it was well past 8:00 a.m. And Chris was officially dissapointed.

"Ah, fuck it," he finally said, walking toward the bathroom. He picked up the porn magazine and smiled. He felt a wave of merriment suddenly take over his body as the smoke began to clear and the centerfold flipped out, exposing a long-legged blonde wearing only a Santa's hat.

Chris pulled a cigarette from the pack and flicked the lighter. He closed the bathroom door, leaving the chaos behind, and began to sing, "Oh cum all ye faithful, joyful and triumphant..."

Housefires blazed throughout the neighborhood as stars glowed red and blue and green, blinking in strange sequences.

# BETHLEHEM: 9 MONTHS B.C.

L ittle Solomon looked across the field full of tiny lights
glowing in the twilight. Lightning bugs drifted in the
wind, signaling in flight. In the distance, he saw Jonas
smiling and waving.

"Come here, Solomon. I have something to show you."

Solomon stopped petting the tiny mouse he had found in
a rotted limb which had fallen during the last storm. He
placed the mouse back into its burrow and met Jonas at the
center of the field.

Jonas slipped off his sandals and motioned for Solomon
to follow him. They ran, chasing fireflies, laughing and
dancing to the sound of the wind through the trees.

After tiring they sat next to a large rock in the tall grass
and stared at the darkening sky.

"Do you want to see something neat?" Jonas asked.

Solomon shook his head, noticing the palm of Jonas'
hand illuminated by a single firefly. The insect climbed atop
Jonas' knuckle, preparing to take flight until Jonas cupped
his other hand over its body.

"Let it go," Solomon said.

A dark glare washed over Jonas' face as he pinched the bug between his thumb and index finger. A white bead of liquid bubbled from behind the insect's wing.

"You're killing it," Solomon yelled, "Stop it!"

"No," Jonas returned.

Solomon grabbed at his palm as Jonas squeezed harder.

"Watch," Jonas said as he raked the bug's body over the face of the rock. A trail of yellow light fell behind the insect's deteriorating body. Jonas hooked the illuminated trail until a "J" appeared on the rock.

"Only four more to complete my name."

Little Solomon felt like smacking Jonas, but instead turned and walked away.

Suddenly the wind gusted and howled and Jonas screamed.

Solomon whirled to see Jonas' feet taken out from under him as his body was lifted into the air. Solomon focused on the expression of fear on Jonas' face. His thin, wiry body rose then suddenly stopped. His head snapped back. His eyes bulged from some unseen force of pressure

The invisible force lowered him, scraping his head across the earth next to the rock. Face down, Jonas' neck went limp, his mouth gaped until streaks of blood and brains steadily spewed atop the grass, like permanent ink from a marker. The trail of blood twisted and looped until it spelled something.

Solomon watched as Jonas' lifeless body was then discarded into the tall grass as the wind settled to a slight breeze.

Solomon looked to the sky, but saw nothing but moon and stars.

******

A little boy looked down at Solomon from beyond the clouds as a booming voice suddenly interrupted his amusement.

"Are you playing with humans again?"

The boy tucked his chin against his chest and shied away from the unseen voice overhead.

"What did I tell you about that?"

The boy looked up, cringing. "I'm sorry, Father. It won't happen again."

"How would you like it if I sent you down there as one of them?"

The little boy's eyes widened as he lowered his head. "Oh no, Father. I wouldn't."

The voice returned, echoing around him. "Next time you disobey me, Jesus, I'm sending you down there as an infant. And then you'll see how it is to be a mere human."

Jesus glanced down to earth and saw the trail of blood scrawling the letters: ESUS. Disappointed that the J on the rock had lost its glow, Jesus glanced up in search of his father. He whispered his name, but no reply came.

Jesus smiled and set his sights on the field where Solomon was looking down at the body of Jonas. He pulled Solomon's body off the ground and, with one swoop, Jesus painted the rock with a J and quickly disposed of the human's body.

Jesus stared down at his drawing as his father's voice yelled at him from above. "I warned you, little one! Now you will have to face the consequences."

Before Jesus could beg or argue, he found himself lodged in a warm place of fluids and darkness. He felt his features in the darkness, noticing the solid wall of human flesh now covering his entire body. He wiggled blindly amongst the fluid and pushed against the elastic edges of his confinement, but found himself trapped, awaiting his release.

# FALLEN

The first thing Rikki saw when he walked outside in the morning was his dog, Pete, darting after a squirrel. As the squirrel cleared the roadway, Pete didn't make it. A car slammed on its brakes, smashing the dog's skull into the pavement. Blood gushed across the pavement, bones snapped, echoing off the asphalt. Rikki cringed, running toward the road, but it was too late. As the car sped off, his dog, Pete, lay behind, his twisted and broken body lurching one last time to smear blood onto Rikki's shoe.

Rikki collapsed next to his dog and cried. Then he ran off into the field behind his house and cried some more.

Only minutes after moving into the field, he saw something in the air. It soared, plummeting fast toward the earth. Rikki stared through blurred vision, wiping tears from his eyes. The white object continued to drop as it finally bounced off the ground and squealed.

Rikki ran over to where it had landed and gasped, noticing that it was a fallen angel, its wings broken badly. Rikki was astonished by its simple beauty. Its feathery, white wings extended on both sides, gently flexing. Its naked body appeared to be both male and female, with a hint of breasts and firm buttocks, a broad muscular chest and wide hips. Its golden hair was short and choppy, the face plain with unblinking eyes as blue as the sky. Between the angel's legs appeared blonde, silky hair that covered a slight parting of the skin that appeared to be a vagina.

Rikki felt ashamed to feel his penis grow stiff at the sight. Especially since the creature was obviously in distress. He quickly shifted his pants around and knelt next to it.

"Are you okay?"

The angel didn't speak, just stared with its blue eyes.

"Wait here," Rikki said, "I'll go get the wagon."

Rikki returned minutes later with the wagon. He loaded the angel and wheeled it back to the house.

\*\*\*\*\*\*

His stepfather dropped his can of beer at the first sight of Rikki's angel.

"What the fuck?" he said, cocking his head to get a better view.

His mother gasped at the sight. "No way, mister. You're not bringing home another pet!"

"But Mom—"

"You heard me," she replied, pointing him back toward the door.

"It's not a pet, it's an angel and it's hurt."

His mother approached it and her eyes suddenly gleamed with that same maternal look as when Rikki would skin his knees while playing ball.

"Oh my," she said, "Let's go bandage up this poor creature's wings and put some Bactine on that cut!"

His stepfather just stared up and down the creature's body.

\*\*\*\*\*\*

Reverend Tanner called after hearing the news. He told Rikki that he must turn the angel over to the church before something bad happened. He also rambled on about some book and ancient prophecy that stated that God would deliver an angel onto the earth to test mankind. If the angel was cared for, then mankind would be saved from God's wrath, but, if this angel was to perish, then mankind would perish as well.

Rikki didn't listen to the preacher. He knew the real reason the angel had come. It was to take Pete to heaven. But somehow it had fallen.

******

Rikki arranged half of his room to keep the angel secure. He pulled out the air mattress and piled blankets around the floor so that the angel could rest and heal its wings.

Thunder echoed outside as twilight had fallen. Lightning lifted the gloom from time to time as the angel just sat amid the nest of blankets and stared at Rikki. From time to time, it would shift around uncomfortably, trying to maneuver out of the patchwork gauze his mother had wrapped around its mummified wings.

A crash of lightning sent Rikki to the window. Rain pelted his bedroom window as he stared out into the street...

...And noticed Pete still lying beside the road, alone. Forgotten.

Sadness gripped Rikki as he remembered all the good times with his faithful companion. He already felt the first rush of tears as night had fallen and Pete's usual place at the end of his bed was empty.

The angel stared at Rikki, devoid of emotion.

Outside the rain fell harder. Rikki noticed cars passing Pete, splashing his body by the side of the road. Guilt gnawed at Rikki until he gave in to it and searched for his raincoat.

His father peeked around the door. He tilted the can of beer to his mouth, then said, "You're not going out there now, are you?"

Rikki nodded and continued, buttoning his raincoat.

"I'll take care of your pet while you take care of the dog."

**I'LL BE DAMNED | 90**

Rikki hesitated momentarily, feeling uncomfortable about leaving, but then guilt hammered away once again and he departed.

******

The rain was cold as Rikki trudged through the yard with a bag and shovel. As he approached the street, Pete suddenly rose, turning to face him.
"Oh my God," Rikki said quietly to himself. "Pete?"
The dog stared back with coal-black eyes. Its eroded face clicked with broken bones as it growled hollowly in Rikki's direction. Blood and internal juices trickled from its caved-in mouth. It lashed out at Rikki, almost biting his arm, then scurried off into the darkness, running on its hind legs. It was the strangest sight Rikki had ever witnessed.

The day was like a bad nightmare and little did Rikki know that this nightmare had just began. For when he returned to his room, the angel was spread eagle across his bed. His stepfather was smoking a cigarette beside it, his boxers around his ankles, his erection only beginning to fade.

******

The rest of the night, the angel rocked back and forth continually. Rikki noticed the slit between its leg had expanded thanks to his stepfather. Reverend Tanner's discussion suddenly bothered him, taking in the events of the night. First his dog had returned from the dead with solid black eyeballs, then his father rapes the angel. Things weren't looking good for mankind.

And so much for Rikki's theory on why the angel had come to earth. It sure as hell wasn't for Pete, especially now that he was some kind of zombified demon-dog.

Rikki suddenly felt the weight of existence pressing down on him. Pressing harder and harder until he finally fell fast asleep.

******

SHANE RYAN STALEY / 91

T he next day Rikki kept the angel locked in his room. Despite protecting it from his stepfather, he also had to protect it from Pete, especially now since his parents had let the dog back into the house.

Rikki couldn't understand why his parents didn't show any concern about a dead dog suddenly reappearing at their doorstep, begging for Gravy Train. And how could anyone not notice that Pete now walked on his hind legs, dragging a three-foot strand of intestines behind his rear end? Something was indeed very wrong here.

Morning passed to afternoon. Rikki locked himself in the room with the angel as it still rocked back and forth non-stop, aggravated and scared.

Rikki's mom knocked on the door and announced Reverend Tanner had come to see him.

Rikki peeked around the corner and saw the Reverend standing in the doorway. He looked back at the angel and slipped out of his bedroom door.

"Hello, son. I've come to see the angel."

"I'm keeping it," Rikki said, glancing back down the hallway where darkness loomed. He glanced around the living room, looking for Pete, but saw no trace.

"I don't think that is wise," Reverend Tanner explained, "If something were to happen to it, mankind would surely perish."

Rikki's stepfather suddenly belched in the living room as the television echoed of a woman in mid-orgasm. Reverend Tanner shifted uncomfortably, then looked around Rikki.

"Is it back there?"

"Nope," Rikki replied.

His mother suddenly cut in. "Now Rikki don't lie! Hasn't Reverend Tanner told you that you'll go to hell for that?" Rikki rolled his eyes, looking back at his bedroom door.

And he found that it had suddenly opened.

He also noticed the large chunk of organ that had fallen off in the hallway.

## I'LL BE DAMNED / 92

"Oh shit!" Rikki said.

His mother gasped. "Rikki!"

But he had already headed for his room. Once there, he pushed the door open to the sight of Pete lying at the end of his bed. Feathers floated everywhere. A mass of bloody tissue mixed with feathers coated the pile of blankets.

"Oh shit!" Reverend Tanner repeated, looking in.

His mother and stepfather peeked in as well.

"Honey, go get the Wet and Dry Shop-Vac, please."

"God dammit!" his stepfather said, "I told you he wasn't responsible enough for another pet!"

"You never said a damn thing!"

"Bull Shit! I did too. He can clean up the mess. I'm going to the liquor store."

"Oh sure," his mother yelled, "You always go to the liquor store when things go wrong."

"Yeah, yeah. Shut the fuck up."

Rikki glanced over at Reverend Tanner to see that his face was stark white and sad, his eyes dark. Darker than normal.

The Reverend walked away as Rikki followed him to the door. Outside his mother and father were shouting over the howling wind. The mid-afternoon sun had vanished. The streetlights kicked on as a massive black sheet of smoke began covering the sky. The temperature suddenly became unbearably hot. Birds dropped in mid-flight, crashing into the ground.

Pete approached on his hind legs, stopped suddenly and latched onto the Reverend's leg, pumping wildly.

Rikki's stepfather flipped his mother off and peeled out of the drive, heading for the liquor store. The sheet of darkness expanded overhead, spinning in a vortex, sucking at the earth.

As the void drew closer, the familiar sound of the local ice cream truck echoed through the darkness. Rikki squinted into the darkness, waiting for the small truck to emerge. *I could use a nice cold bomb-pop right about now,* he thought.

# CASWELL

The mid-afternoon sun glinted off the vine-shrouded windows of the ancient house. It stood away from the road with a black wrought iron fence, almost swallowed by weeds, coiling a reptilian path into the back yard where the twilight cast strange shadows and a pair of gleaming eyes disappearing into the overgrowth.

Then Timothy felt his mother's hand gripping the small of his neck, firmly steering him through the gate, across the lawn and up the steps to the door.

The porch was fit for the house. Smashed flies coated the screen door, a dead pigeon lay on the welcome mat and, in a corner, a white mouse slumped in the back of a toy dump truck with a miniature football helmet wedged on its head. Yet his mother noticed nothing unusual.

"Ring the doorbell," she said, releasing him.

"But we were just here a couple months ago!" Timothy pleaded, his small hand hesitating before the lighted button. Behind him, he heard the fence blow shut.

"Just go play with your cousin and have fun!"

"But I hate Lance!" Timothy replied. "Him and all his creatures. He's a weirdo!"

His own words suddenly triggered the memory of the red-haired, red-freckled scrawny boy stationed in the back yard's jungle-like terrain along with the creatures, God so many creatures: the garden snake down his back, the mouse in his Kool-Aid, and the salamander in his swimming trunks.

"There's nothing wrong with him!" his mother recited. "Lance is a good kid." It was the adorable kid lecture again. "If you don't get along, I'll have Grandma give you an extra pinch or two!"

Timothy's mind shifted onto another horrible memory: his grandma tugging and wiggling on his cheeks. His face numbed in anticipation.

"I'll get along, but I'm not going to like him!"

"Good! Now are you going to ring that doorbell or do *I* have to?"

"I already—"

"You did not!" his mother shouted. "Now ring it!"

Timothy jabbed at the doorbell hoping that it was out of order, but a low-pitched chime echoed inside. His body stiffened as he heard footsteps nearing the door.

His grandmother opened the door, smiled and reached for him, her hands white with baking powder. Before he could react, she had a firm grip on his cheek, slowly pulling apart the suction-bond between his skin and gums.

"Hello there....come in, let me see how much you've grown!" His grandmother pulled him into her apron, but he quickly squirmed free and set his sights beyond her large frame for a lurking figure with a sunburnt face. So far there were no signs.

"Go say hi to your grandpa!" His grandmother pointed him into the living room where he saw the old man slumped in a recliner, his head tucked into his chest, eyes closed.

Timothy suddenly stopped, his heart plummeting as the evil grin appeared. Lance was sitting beside him!

Timothy crossed his eyes slightly, so that the vision blurred into a red splotch in the periphery, then continued.

"Hi Grandpa," Timothy said, tapping on his knee. His grandpa didn't move.

"Grandpa!" Timothy yelled. Still no reply, not even a sign

of movement.

"Grandpa's dead!" Lance said, grinning malevolently.

"He is not!" Timothy replied.

"He is too. Just ask Bill," Lance said as he leaned towards his grandfather and blew on a patch of grey hair peeking from his ear.

"Who's Bill?"

"This is Bill!" Lance said as he pulled the mangled centipede from his shirt pocket. It squirmed helplessly, flipped over, then quit moving between Lance's bony fingers. "He's my pet!"

"How's he gonna tell me anything?" Timothy asked, taking a step back.

"Just watch." Lance shoved the centipede into his grandfather's ear and cupped his hand over it. The spiky-haired worm clung to the earlobe before he scooped its wriggling body and tossed it back in the ear canal. He withdrew his hand and it was gone. "If he comes back, it means that Grandpa's okay, but if he don't — Grandpa's dead and Bill's found a new home."

"How do *you* know?" asked Timothy.

"I told him I would squash him if he doesn't do as I say!" Lance said, slamming his fist into his palm.

Timothy waited for the worm, but nothing appeared. Could his grandfather really be dead? He looked into his wrinkled face, beneath every sag without seeing the slightest twitch. Had the line between Lance's games and reality finally vanished?

"Come here!" Timothy motioned to his mother who was walking through the room. "Is Grandpa dead?"

"He's just sleeping, silly!" She shook her head and laughed, disappearing into the kitchen as his grandpa finally snored.

Timothy furiously retreated to the kitchen as Lance trailed.

"Come outside, I've got something to show you." Lance stated.

I'LL BE DAMNED | 96

"What is it?" Timothy moved next to his mother at the sink.

"It's a secret, Tim." His aunt, Betty, leaned over the counter flashing a toothless smile. "Lance has got a million secrets around here. He wants you to go see for yourself."

What could it be this time? Another snake? A dead rabbit? Or maybe he decided to drag a whole cow off the neighbor's farm. God only knew what the back yard concealed.

"I don't want to," Timothy replied. His mother turned her head immediately and he knew what the look on her face meant. He had no choice, he had to go.

Timothy waded through the knee-high grass to the back of the property where an old wood shed stood, seeming to float on all kinds of plant life. The grass was trampled in paths which dissected the yard, each channel seemed to run to and from the dilapidated building. Timothy could tell that Lance spent most of his time there because the yard looked like his own personal junk yard with old rain-soaked blankets, rusted toys, and even tattered clothes strung across and half-buried in the thick crabgrass.

Lance knelt before an enormous stack of firewood which overlapped the edge of the shed. He pulled a strange plant from the ground and handed it to Timothy.

"Smells like rabbit piss, don't it?"

Timothy lowered his nose and cringed as Lance shoved the plant into his face, stood back, and laughed hysterically.

"What'd you do that for?" Timothy asked, wiping his mouth.

"It's poison ivy!"

"But you touched it."

"So I don't get poison ivy, do you?" Lance doubled over, his face flushed into a uniform color with his hair as he pointed his finger at Timothy and covered his mouth, muffling the laughter.

"Is that what I came out here to see?"

"Nope, it's under the shed!" Lance's face quickly

contracted into an emotionless gaze as Timothy's caution grew. He knew there was something waiting nearby.

"What's under there?"

"Come here and I'll show you!" Lance squatted and pointed to a burrow dug beneath the shed's door.

"No way," Timothy replied. "There's probably more skunks or a big snake or something!"

"Fine! Be a scared-e-cat then!" Lance sneered. "It's just Caswell!"

"What's Caswell?"

"A monster."

"Oh, like the stuffed giraffe-monster in your closet or the one that wore your mom's underwear on its head?"

"No! I'm talking about a real monster!"

The deck door suddenly swung open and Uncle Jim stepped out with a spatula in his hand. "Come and get it, boys. "Your dogs are cooked and served!"

*Hopefully he was talking about hot dogs,* Timothy thought.

After supper, Lance sat on his grandmother's lap, putting on his regular act: showing off and lying his way to be the center of everyone's attention.

"Grandma, you want to see my pet monster?" Lance asked.

"Oh, you have a pet monster, do you? I'd love to meet it!" his grandma replied.

"Don't let it get you now!" His grandpa mumbled, awaking briefly to scratch in his ear.

Timothy sat on the deck as he watched Lance and his grandma walking toward the shed.

"Show off!" Timothy whispered.

His grandmother laughed as she pointed beneath the shed. "Hello Mr. Caswell, how are you today?"

Then the childish game ended and she screamed. Her large body plummeted to the ground. Her hands frantically scraped the dirt but to no avail as her body was slowly pulled toward the shed.

Timothy gasped as he watched her flowered dress rip apart as her body was sucked into the hole.

Timothy's heart raced as he waited for his grandmother to emerge.

Lance stood silently holding his arms out. "Whoops. Caswell got her!" he remarked, kneeling to peer beneath the shed.

As the cloud of dust settled, Timothy saw more movement.

"Grandma!" he yelled as he ran toward the shed.

Timothy cleared the woodpile, seeing Lance's hands clamped onto the door, his body lodged beneath the shed.

Timothy stood there watching him struggle.

"Help me...please!" Lance's scream mutated into a grunt as the wood trim splintered, breaking his grip. He flailed wildly, attempting to roll away from the hole, but he was held there until finally his body was jerked beneath the shed.

After Lance had disappeared, Timothy's gaze lifted and he found himself grinning, but then he remembered his grandma was down there too.

Timothy ran to the house, threw back the deck door, and shouted, "Mom, come quick! Something got Grandma and pulled her into a hole!"

Aunt Betty laughed, turning toward his mother. "These kids have imaginations like you wouldn't believe."

"No, she....fell under the shed......she's hurt!"

The police arrived an hour later to discover the tunnel. Something had burrowed from the shed to the crawlspace where they found his grandma's remains.

Lance, in a fit of seizure, was curled next to her.

******

Months passed and Timothy returned to the house. He walked around the property searching the back yard for movement. The door opened and Aunt Betty peaked out. "Well, there you are. I was wondering

SHANE RYAN STALEY / 99

when you were going to get here."

Timothy entered the house and sat next to Lance.

"Hi Lance," Timothy whispered. Lance's hollow eyes gazed ahead at nothing, his body slouching lifelessly in the wheelchair.

"It's no use, Tim. He's still catatonic. We've been taking him to therapy each week with that other kid, Jason Milton, but neither of them have made any progress."

Timothy remembered Jason Milton as the nerdy kid who stole his crayons and sniffed glue. One weekend, he was comatose in some kind of accident and his teacher made each class member send him a card. On Jason's card, Timothy drew a stick-figure with thick glasses and a glue bottle wedged up his nose.

Aunt Betty cleared her throat, interrupting Timothy's memory. "I'm going to go see Doctor Murphy about Lance. Just keep an eye on him while I'm gone. Help yourself to the T.V. and any snacks you want."

"Thanks, I will," Timothy replied.

"I talked to your mother today. She says you're still having trouble with that bully at school. What's his name?"

"Billy Brewer," Timothy replied, his face flushing. His mother had probably told the whole town he'd been beaten up three times in the past week by Big-Bad Billy alone.

Aunt Betty grabbed her purse and waddled through the doorway. "Just ignore him and he probably won't bother you. Well, I'm going to be late.....bye, bye now!"

Timothy stared at Lance, waving his hands across the boy's face. He knew Lance wouldn't be going anywhere.

Timothy looked out the window toward the shed. Long blades of grass stirred silently in the wind. It almost felt peaceful. He looked back upon Lance, then walked out to the burrow.

The hole had partially caved in. Timothy scooped handfuls of dirt away from the shed's door when he first smelled the stench of urine.

Something scurried closer to the door. Timothy stood

back, seeing a shape shifting in the darkness, its eyes almost glowing.

"Caswell?" Timothy knelt to get a better look. A flurry of dust arose from the hole as he stared down into the darkness. "You can come out now. I've found you a new home."

Timothy giggled as it emerged from the hole and stood on two feet. Its bloated flesh was dirty and scabbed, possessing an odor of a wet dog.

"But you've been bad!" Timothy shouted, pointing his finger at its four heads. "You shouldn't have eaten Grandma too!" Its body momentarily retracted. A weeping yellow stream dripped onto the grass.

"Now let her go right now!"

Suddenly the thing's body convulsed. Its mouth slowly opened, belching a clear silhouette into the air.

Timothy watched his grandma's silhouette drift upward and vanish.

"Good boy!" Timothy said, patting its three remaining heads. The exposed yellow-eyed, ill-formed head in the middle lifted to his touch, but the other two human-faced heads wriggled violently, held captive by a thin membrane of hairless skin.

Timothy looked closer at the two, watching the silhouette-faces of Lance and Jason Milton struggle to poke through.

*There's plenty of room now that Grandma's gone,* Timothy thought as he led Caswell down the twisting back road toward Billy Brewer's house.

# THE SMOKER

The sky darkened as the bus made its way into the city. Steven Ford watched a shadow cross his magazine as the ocean of pavement washed around the bus filling the morning scenery with bumper to bumper traffic. He sighed, his body tensing, as he realized how much he had enjoyed his trip to the countryside. No big-city traffic, no commotion, no swarms of rude people filtering to the same destinations.

But now he was headed back to work from his week-long vacation, back to the job and city he hated. Steven thought about calling in sick, but his work would only pile higher.

The bus stopped as new passengers crowded on the bus. An old man sat across from him, his leathery face twitching as he watched Steven out of the corner of his eye.

Steven cringed, turning to look out the window where dreary buildings loomed over a small church on the corner. A swarm of pedestrians eclipsed the littered pavement in front of the church. In the distance, a gloom-stricken factory's smoke stack spewed forth a mixture of black and grey smog coating the horizon.

The sun disappeared.

The bus turned the corner as the old man across from Steven shifted to one side, pulling out a case from his suit pocket.

Steven glanced over, catching a strange glimmer in his

eye. Grey stubble, similar to the tiny grey hairs atop his head, coated his face. His eyes were dark and roaming through the crowded bus until they met Steven's.

Steven looked away as the man stared back in his direction. When he glanced back, the man flipped open the case, pulled out a short black cigar, and chewed off one of the ends. Once in his mouth, the man lit the cigar and inhaled. A puff of black smoke swirled in the air, soon thinning into a layer which floated towards Steven.

Steven held his breath as the smoke drifted, burning his nose, watering his eyes.

"Do you mind?" Steven asked, pointing to the *NO SMOKING* sign in front of the bus.

The man shook his head, took in another deep breath of smoke and exhaled.

"Sir, please," a thin, bucktoothed woman whispered. "Not around my baby."

Others sitting around him placed their attention towards the cigar.

The man held out his index finger and inhaled again. Then he exhaled, blowing out a mass of black smoke. The smoke drifted shortly, swirling into a circle. The circle grew, splitting off into two congruent spheres.

"Oh wow!" a young boy said, "do it again."

The old man smiled.

Steven shifted his body away from the man. As he looked back, all eyes were staring in awe as the man blew out another ring which drifted over to the lady with the small baby. The black smoke ring settled against her earlobe.

A skinny man in a dark suit pointed, "An earring!"

The crowd erupted in laughter and cheers.

"Hey," Steven said, barely holding back his anger. "Please put out the cigar. You might choke up her baby."

The woman covered her child's face. "Oh, don't worry. He'll be fine. Go on!"

"What's wrong with you people?" Steven yelled, though nobody paid any attention.

The smoker lifted the cigar back to his lips and sucked in a breath full. This time, another ring drifted from his mouth, towards a small boy. As it rolled through the air, tiny tentacles of smoke spread from the outline, forming what looked to be seams on a baseball.

The ball of smoke rolled closer, smacking the boy in the face. Blood gushed from his nose and mouth.

"How terrible of you," an old woman said, rushing to the boy's aid.

The old man's eyes gleamed with amusement. He took in another breath and blew out a thick rectangular mass of smoke. The rectangle soon formed into a shadowy bird. Wings flapped into motion, circling the old woman.

The old woman screamed as the bird-like outline dove into her face. Her glasses fell to the floor. A bloody gash formed upon her cheek. She sobbed wildly as the crowd panicked.

"Stop the bus, " somebody yelled.

The bus finally pulled over as everyone rushed to exit.

But Steven sat motionless, his hands slowly clenching into fists. He turned toward the man and stared. "You're not going to push *me* around," he said. "I'm sick and tired of everyone in the city making my life hell!"

The smoker said nothing as the bus departed once again.

Steven returned his gaze out the window until he heard the man gasping for a breath. Steven turned to see him blow out a thick stream of black smoke into his face.

Steven tried to move away, but the smoke encased him, squeezing the sides of his head.

Steven struggled, shaking his head. The smoke parted as he opened his eyes seeing a number of rings linked together as a chain which pressed against his face. Steven felt his face numb as he reached for the window. Quickly, he pulled the window down and stuck his head out. The black chain crumbled into the air.

Steven returned, staring at the man, his cigar burnt to a nub.

The man toked intensely at the remainder of the cigar. Inhaling, a faint smirk appeared on the man's face as he spit out a tiny puff of smoke.

The smoke quickly transformed into the shape of a bullet, rapidly drifting toward Steven.

Steven lunged forward as the bullet of smoke sped by, shattering the window.

The bus slowed, the driver cursed and glared.

A bead of sweat trickled down Steven's face. He felt his cheeks and forehead burning with rage.

"That's it! I've had it!" Steven yelled, reaching into his back pocket, pulling out a can. He quickly emptied the entire can into his mouth, stuffing the contents to one side of his cheek.

The man squinted at Steven, confused.

Steven filtered some of the substance into his lower lip, then leaned into the aisle and spit a black wad onto the man's seat.

The man frowned, looking beside him.

Suddenly the clump moved, slowly spreading itself out to a long slender rope-like projection, tapering to a slender point. The particles hardened into a solid shape.

The man slid away from the moving mass, realizing what it had become.

A tiny flickering tongue extended from the diamond-shaped head as its body slithered towards the man.

Steven watched the sheer terror in the man's eyes as the snake-like mass wrapped itself around his neck and constricted,

The man struggled, pulling at the body, his legs kicked against the seat, his mouth gasping for air.

His face turned blue, the veins bulging in his neck.

His head jerked back as his body went limp, momentarily twitching, then nothing.

The black mass slowly broke apart, crumbling down the man's shirt, onto the floor.

Steven sat back, crossed his legs, and opened the

magazine to the vacation section.

"I've got to get away from all of this," he mumbled to himself as the bus rolled onward approaching his exit.

# THE ROAD TRIP

The car sputtered slightly in the drive as Bob stomped on the gas, tearing through gravel.

His wife screamed from the front porch, "Go to hell, asshole!"

Bob slammed his fist against the steering wheel as he turned onto a country road. This was his normal ritual when the fights broke out: take a lap through the countryside to calm his temper then return to the couch for a long night ahead. Otherwise, he would beat his wife, end up in jail, and go through another year of counseling. And Bob knew he didn't have the money to go through that again.

Each new trip, Bob took a new route, discovering a new part of the countryside he had never seen before. Sometimes he felt like he had traveled to a new world. The night soothed his anger, and the landscape ignited his delusions of living in happy times.

Bob slowed the car to fifty-five as he hit a dirt road. Corn lined both sides of the roadway. Dilapidated barns stood firmly in fields as his headlights caught flashes of eyes reflecting from grazing cattle or pigs swimming in mud holes.

The smell of manure wafted through his car.

Bob took in a deep breath and thought about how much he had wanted to move to the country. Farm the land. Raise livestock. Be his own boss. And be free of the hectic city life, a monotonous day job at the factory, and the woman who had trapped him into the lifestyle he so detested.

Bob drove over hills, beside fields, going farther than he had ever gone before. Finally the country dirt roads faded to a narrow paved channel.

"Where the hell am I?" Bob whispered to himself.

The reflection of a green and white sign caught Bob's attention. The first signs of a small town came into view as houses and parked cars littered the scenery.

Bob squinted as the headlights shone on the sign. He waited for the sign to come into focus so he could read the name of the town.

Finally the blurred white words fused into something he could read: HELL.

*What kind of town is named Hell?*

Curious, Bob continued as a bigger square sign came into view.

*Welcome to Hell,* the sign said, *A rapidly growing community.*

Bob shook his head and read the next line: *Visit our library.*

A barber's shop appeared with a red and blue swirling sign glowing through the darkness. A neon sign read: *DEVIL'S HAIRCUT SPECIAL!!!, only $6.66 with the purchase of a comb.*

Bob watched an old drunken man stumble along the sidewalk next to the fire station. As the man continued, flames suddenly shot up through a crack in the asphalt. The man dropped to his knees. Flames clung to his weathered jacket. The man curled into a fetal position as his skin bubbled.

Bob stopped the car, staring in disbelief. *Where are the firemen? Police Officers? Why isn't anyone helping this man?*

Bob opened the door and stepped upon the roadway. Smoke drifted from the soles of his shoes. His laces caught fire.

The old man, still smoldering, stood once again and

entered another bar.

Bob hopped back into his car. The smell of burning rubber drifted in his window.

He glanced into the fire station, noticing there were people staring out each of the windows of the giant garage door where the fire engines were. Each face cringed horribly as Bob heard a long chorus of blood-curdling screams shaking the windows where people clawed frantically, fingerprints of blood streaking the glass.

Down the street, more flames erupted along the roadway. A body tumbled across the sidewalk.

Bob locked the doors and reached for the cellular phone in the back seat.

After fumbling with the buttons, he finally dialed his home number.

His wife answered, "Hello."

"Marge, thank God you answered."

"Bob is that you? Where are you calling from?"

Bob hesitated, looking back down the roadway. "Oh Marge, I'm in Hell."

"Oh, honey," she said, "I am too. I'm so sorry for those awful things I said to you. Please come—."

"No, you don't understand," Bob said. "I *am* in Hell. You know the place of burning souls, gnashing teeth — eternal damnation."

His wife paused, then exhaled a deep breath. "Have you been drinking again?"

"No!" Bob yelled. "I'm serious. I swear on Josh's life — I'm in hell!"

"Oh my God," she replied. "Did you get in a car accident?"

Bob leaned his head against the steering wheel, gently banging his forehead. "How in the world would I be able to talk to you if I'm dead?"

"I guess you've got a point," his wife said, "Then how exactly did you end up there?"

"I was just driving the back roads when I came to this

town!"

"So it's only a town named Hell—"

"No!" Bob screamed. "It *is* a town, but it's the real Hell. There's flames shooting around the road, people are screaming."

Suddenly the back end of the car sunk.

"Just a minute."

Bob opened the door and glanced behind him, realizing the tires had melted away.

Bob slammed the door shut, picked up the phone. A dog trotted beside the car, its tail aflame.

"Wow, there's even dogs here!"

"So what are you going to do?" his wife asked.

"I don't really know," Bob replied. "There's no place to turn around and my tires have melted."

Sweat beaded upon his forehead from the sweltering heat radiating from beneath the car.

Bob glanced around as the dog returned, dragging a woman across the roadway by her hair. More dogs appeared from a dark alleyway, running to the woman. The pack settled chewing her apart, limb by limb.

Bob gagged.

His wife's voice shot through the receiver: "Honey, are you okay, are you there?"

"I'm still here."

"Oh, I'm so sorry you're in this mess," his wife said. "But remember it could always be worse."

*I guess I could have ended up in L.A.*, Bob thought.

"Hold on a second, dear," his wife said, "I have another call on the line."

The phone clicked.

*Christ, this is going to be one hell of a phone bill*, Bob thought as a body suddenly fell from the sky, bouncing across the sidewalk in front of an antique store. Flames engulfed the body as it crawled into a storm drain.

His wife's voice erupted once again. "Bob, it's Charlotte. She's having trouble with Frank again. I told her I'd call her right back."

Bob slumped in the seat as headlights flashed in his rearview mirror. Slowly a black Lincoln town car pulled behind him, flashing its lights and honking its horn.

"I've got to go," Bob said, disgusted, "Some asshole wants to pass me."

"Okay dear. Do you think you'll be home in time for breakfast?"

Bob hung the phone up, stuck his arm out the window, waving the car on.

Slowly it coasted beside him. A tinted window rolled down as Bob saw a strange man wearing a backwards baseball cap.

"You lost?" the man asked.

"Sure am. How do you get out of this place?"

The man smiled. "Dead end up ahead. You got to back your way out of here."

"I can't," Bob stated, "my tires are gone."

"Shame," the man said, taking off his baseball cap to reveal a set of ivory horns. "Now I'm gonna have to eat you."

Bob floored it in reverse. Sparks shot from the tires. Veering from one side of the road to the other, Bob continued as the black car soon faded into the distance.

A couple miles down the road, Bob noticed a town coming into view. He drove faster in reverse until he came upon a car in the middle of the road. A black Lincoln town car.

Bob managed to back next to the car. The tinted windows rolled down once again.

Bob leaned out the window. "Are you really going to eat me?"

The devil laughed. "I was just joking. That only happens in the eighth level."

Flames shot around the car as Bob felt the hairs on his arms and legs curling.

Once again he floored the car in reverse, soon meeting the same black car in the road.

SHAME RYAN STALEY / 111

Bob stopped, looked around.  He glanced back down the road as the pavement receded into sheer darkness.

The thought of returning to his wife suddenly troubled him.  Even if he could escape, he'd have to return to another situation he wanted to escape from.

Bob shook his head.  "Dammit," he yelled.

*At least they have a bar here*, he thought as he shut off the engine.  *The beer's probably warm, but I bet the women are wild!*

He motioned to the devil.  "Can I at least have a drink before I get scorched?"

The devil nodded.  "Sure.  It's on me."

Bob stepped out of the car.  Flames swirled around him, catching his hair on fire.  Slowly the flames danced around his body, blistering his flesh.  A massive throbbing pain branched throughout his entire body, pulsing each second a thought went through his mind or a muscle in his body twitched.

Through the screams and the crackling of his own flesh, he still heard the devil laugh and say, "Whoops."

# BURNT OFFERING

I stared at the joint, still finding it hard to believe. It had been rolled six times, contained six seeds spaced evenly throughout all six grams of black pot. Gabriel sealed it back up after making these observations, his bloodshot eyes meeting mine with the same look of hesitance.

"What do you think?" he asked, "should we smoke it?"

"Where did you say you got it?"

"The Arcade Man gave it to me. He said it was one hell of a high!"

Suddenly I felt cautious about the situation. Anyone known as "The Arcade Man" should have rang a warning bell in my head, or literally a buzzer telling me to abandon any further progression. But instead I just nodded and simply shrugged my shoulders. To fuse such a link between thought and action (or, in this case, abstinence) would have taken far too many brain cells already on hold for various other activities.

So Gabriel lit the end, inhaled, and passed it to me. The black paper flaked off in ashes and a seed popped, sending a puff of black smoke into the air. Fingers of smoke drifted, swirling in front of the television. Black streaks formed into strange shapes shifting against the current of air. I felt the smoke crawl into my throat, burning its way into my lungs. Instantly I felt a floating sensation and everything moved in slow-motion.

After finishing the joint, I locked my sights on the candle wavering in the half-light. I leaned back on the recliner, my body feeling heavy and numb, and looked over at Gabriel.

He stared ahead, smiling. "Have you ever thought about selling your soul?"

This was a common question frequenting such state of minds, especially towards the end of the bag. I managed to reel my attention back in for a moment to reply, "Sure. Who hasn't?"

Gabriel leaned back on the couch and that's when I saw a man dressed in a black suit and tie, opening a briefcase made of bone.

The man rose from the couch and paced in front of us.

"Good evening, allow me to introduce myself. My name's Bill and I buy and sell things." He handed me a card which read BILL JOHNSON, INDEPENDENT SALESPERSON. 666 Damnation Drive, Christonastick, Massachusetts 00666.

"Nice card," I said, handing it to Gabriel, "but don't you think it's a little obvious?"

Satan smirked. "A little touch of humor always helps in this business."

Gabriel pointed. "You're the—"

Satan held out his hand like he was trying to stop traffic and Gabriel's mouth froze in mid-sentence.

"Do you mind if I let my tail out?"

I shook my head and tried to swallow but my tongue felt like a giant cottonball stuck to the roof of my mouth.

As he reached around, I noticed the giant bulge in his rear. Satan tugged on a velcro patch in the seat of his dress pants, then pulled out his red, pointed tail which swung chaotically.

"Damn, I feel much better."

I looked over at Gabriel who remained stiff and slack-jawed as he watched Satan's every move.

"Let's cut to the chase, guys. Tell me what you want and it's yours for a price...and you both know what it's going to cost you."

Gabriel suddenly broke free from his trance. "Anything?"

"Anything you desire."

Gabriel smiled. "Whatever I picture in my mind I want to happen."

Gabriel's quick response surprised me. Just two days prior, it took him two hours to decide to move off the couch after he had dropped his burning pipe somewhere in the cushions. Finally he figured if he just sat there, he might smother the flames. Or perhaps it was the simple fact that the recliner was on the other side of the room or that he had fallen asleep in the middle of deciding. Anyway, he awoke without eyebrows, but the couch never fully caught fire.

Satan searched his briefcase, extracting a set of documents. "Just sign these in triplicate. The top copy goes to me, the middle is yours, and the last one goes to goodie-two-shoes up there."

Gabriel quickly signed all three.

"There's just a few regulations, nothing major." Satan smiled. "Go ahead...it's done."

"This is going to be cool!" Gabriel said, looking around the apartment.

"Just picture something in your mind and it will happen."

Gabriel focused on the candle, smiling as the flame left the wick and traveled through mid-air until it hovered above Satan. Suddenly it dropped, igniting his puffy, almost Afro-like hairdo. The giant ball of flame quickly receded to the sight of two ivory horns twisting toward the back of his head. The bony growths glowed brightly amidst the black light mounted on a far wall.

"How amusing," Satan mumbled, turning towards me.

I focused away from his gleaming eyes to where his skin had been charred. Out of the corner of my eye I saw Gabriel smiling.

Satan shook his head, turning to face Gabriel again. "What do you think you're doing?"

As he turned, I caught a glimpse of his tail curling tightly against his body.

Gabriel broke down in laughter. "Look Jason, I made him have a little piggy's tail!"

I found myself chuckling, until I looked up to see Satan once again staring back intently.

A million thoughts raced through my mind. Sweat beaded upon my forehead. This was the rest of my life. How was I to avoid the pressure of losing my eternal soul?

Satan's long, rotted nails tapped wildly upon his bone-plated briefcase. Gabriel stared out the window and I wondered what he was thinking. I soon found out as I watched the full moon melt, spilling upon the earth. The stars swarmed through the sky until they finally assembled together in a compact mass forming a naked woman's body spread throughout the otherwise empty sky. Mercury and Mars, combined with a cluster of stars, settled in her Milky Way breasts. Pluto and Jupiter fell to her nipples as Uranus plummeted to the back of her midsection. A black hole circled between her legs.

Gabriel smiled, still concentrating on the dark, midsummer sky.

"What will it be?"

Suddenly inspiration struck. I took a deep breath and replied, "I wish to go to heaven."

Satan slammed his briefcase shut. "Who the hell do you think I am?"

"You said *anything*, right?"

Satan nodded.

"Then I want to go to heaven."

Satan cursed as a figure in a white robe suddenly appeared, sitting cross-legged and meditating in the middle of the living room floor.

Satan turned, sighing in disgust. "Now look what you've done."

I quickly recognized Jesus from the many oil paintings that possessed my mother's room. His traits looked almost exactly the same as his depiction except for the hairy mole on his cheek and the brown goatee in place of the full beard so commonly seen in most Christian drawings. I liked the moderate change, the long sideburns and goatee made him look like a bad-ass, someone who would give you a good skull-fucking if you took his name in vain.

Jesus smiled at me, his eyes deep and kind. "Pray, my child. Help me defeat this beast who seeks to destroy your spirit."

As the black smoke rolled over my mind, I thought back to my childhood trying to remember a favorite bedtime prayer. After inspiration struck I recited, "I pledge allegiance to the flag of the..."

Jesus rolled his eyes and stood before Satan. "How should we settle this one."

Satan reached into his torn suit jacket and pulled out a coin. "Like always...you get heads and I get tails."

"No," Jesus argued. "Let me see the coin."

Satan reluctantly handed it over. Jesus scanned the coin and tossed it to me. I looked it over and noticed both sides were tails.

"How about a good old fist fight," Satan said, rolling up his sleeves.

Jesus shook his head, crossing his arms. "I am a man of peace."

"Shucks," Satan shouted. "Then how about arm wrestling?"

Surprisingly, Jesus agreed.

I cleared the waterbong and ashtrays off the coffee table as their grips soon locked.

"On the count of three—" I said, my heart fluttering against my chest walls.

"No!" Satan shrieked. "Not three! Make it four. Three and seven are my unlucky numbers."

"Okay," I said, "One...two....three....four...Go!"

Jesus grunted, trying to use his one hundred-forty pound frame the best he could. Satan flexed his biceps, pushing his heftier frame into his momentum, but to no avail. For seven days they remained deadlocked, finally agreeing there had to be a better way.

"What about a nice game of cards?" Satan inquired.

Jesus agreed. They moved into the bathroom to gain privacy, so I couldn't help Jesus cheat. After six days, I sent Gabriel into the bathroom to fill me in on the outcome.

Gabriel returned. "Still even."

"What in the hell are they playing?"

"Go Fish," he replied. "They asked me for beer nuts and pretzels. Satan was drinking out of the toilet and Jesus decided to shave his goatee. If you ask me, they're just stalling."

"Bastards," I said, "What are they trying to do — drive me insane. I can't take much more of this. This is my soul, my eternity — I need to know! Plus I haven't worked for over two weeks and the rent is due."

"I'm hungry," Gabriel said, staring at the floor. A mouse streaked by the couch, beneath the coffee table, and out into the middle of the living room. Gabriel smiled, staring intently at the rodent.

Suddenly its legs dropped off and it turned into a Twinkie.

Gabriel picked it off the floor and shoved it into his mouth. I stared in disbelief as a red cream filling oozed from the center.

Finally, on the sixth night, Jesus emerged from the bathroom. I knelt and kissed his hands and feet. "Thank you for saving my soul...I promise no more hookers."

Jesus pushed me away. "Don't get excited, it's not over yet...we were still tied, but I had to quit. Satan has diarrhea and you ran out of toilet paper. I just couldn't take it in there anymore."

Satan staggered from the room, over to the sofa. "Come here, Jesus."

Jesus walked to the edge of the sofa, his sandals crushing beer cans and potato chip bags.

"I'm exhausted and I've been thinking: why are we

wasting our time on this worthless piece of—"

Jesus pointed his finger to silence the Dark One. "One more game."

I took a deep breath to calm my quivering legs. My nerves settled for the moment.

Jesus extended his cupped hand and said, "Paper-Rock-Scissors. One time to determine who gets his soul."

Satan nodded and extended his hand. Both hands went into motion and both displayed the rock symbol.

"Dammit!" Satan yelled. "We tied again. We have better things to do than waste our time on him."

"I agree," Jesus said, glaring at me. "So it shall end here without further judgment."

I sprung from the couch and yelled "wait, you can't do that. What happens when I finally die?"

Jesus looked at Satan and laughed. "You won't ever die and we'll never have to decide!" He hiked his soiled robe up and exited the apartment while Satan crashed on our recliner.

Stricken with this curse of immortality — stuck in this wretched world for all eternity, there was only one thing left to do — smoke another doobie and sleep on it.

\*\*\*\*\*\*

I dreamt a million pipe dreams that night — visions of a thousand years from now, huddled in bed with an attractive rat or kinky reptile, being the last of my kind amongst a kingdom of animals, and lonely as hell. When morning finally came, there were no signs of Satan.

We left the apartment and walked downtown as morning traffic filtered its way down Main Street. I was numb, an endless sense of dread lingered against any positive emotion I attempted to conjure.

"Maybe we were just high and none of that really happened."

"Possible," Gabriel said. "Stoned for thirteen days..."

"Try thinking something about that lady," I said, pointing to a little old lady window shopping down the walkway. I figured if Gabriel could still use his power of thought to make things happen, then we would finally know for sure that the events actually occurred.

Gabriel squinted at the old lady and immediately blood sprayed from her eye sockets. Portions of her skull chipped away as a surge of brain matter, water, and blood exploded against the window. Her legs buckled, her jaw blew apart, as she lay twitching on the pavement.

"I meant a nice thought," I yelled, smacking him on the side of his head.

"Sorry," he replied, "I meant for her to implode, not explode."

The feeling that I was surely fucked finally surfaced.

"It can't be that bad — you're immortal," Gabriel declared as a smirk washed over his face. "I'll trade you any day."

Suddenly there appeared light in the dark tunnel ahead, though I felt somewhat guilty for taking him for the fool that he was. A moment later, I agreed. The only thing Gabriel had to do was think about switching our fates, then he would be the immortal one and I would have his half-baked wish of being able to think things that happen.

Gabriel focused on the switch then climbed up a light pole. He was obviously very excited as he yelled "Hey, look everyone, I'm invincible!" and jumped into mid-day traffic.

Several cars ran over his body followed by a street cleaner which sucked him up and threw him alongside a curb.

I walked over and sat next to his body and asked if he wanted a smoke. I lifted his head, accidentally tearing it loose from his body. I checked for a pulse and found that he was no more.

Confusion poked riddles into my mind. Had I ever been immortal? And, if so, why hadn't the switch taken place?

I searched Gabriel's pockets and found the contract and scanned the first couple of pages. On the second page there was a list of clauses, one being that he could give his wish to another, but could not receive one in return.

I fell back against the cold asphalt and closed my eyes to the commotion of traffic backed up for blocks. I opened my eyes, searching the street to the glow of the arcade where a man in a black trench coat stood.

"The Arcade Man," I whispered, fury scrambling my mind.

I knew I had both kept my curse as well as acquired a new one when the man's head suddenly exploded. Grey matter splashed against the neon *OPEN* sign. His arms and legs ripped off, trading places.

An old man with a cane hobbled by, kicking an arm which protruded from a leg socket. He stood there a moment, scratched his head and glanced over at me.

A spark of anger flickered through me as I watched the cane work its way out of his hands and beat him to the ground. In a flurry of action, the cane then descended, burrowing deeply into his trousers, disappearing into the seat of his pants.

The man's eyes lit up in pain, he raised his head slightly and screamed as my fury peaked.

A hundred different visions shot through my mind as the earth shook, the sky turned black around the sun, and Gabriel's headless body stood and danced to the thunder and lightning. Black smoke rolled over the land, washing away everything until all that remained was a vacant sky and a strip of desolate earth in which I stood in sheer terror.

I panicked, looking into the endless expanse of darkness. As I stood in the void, I wished for the world to return to normal, but my mind kept dwelling on nothingness. And more black smoke descended from the sky, swirling thicker. Only a halo of sun remained.

As the sun flickered to black, I saw another glimmer — a recollection forming before my eyes. In the void, stars returned in the form of a naked woman's body which glittered, black smoke swirling in forbidden places, reminding me of how alone I was and how desperately I

wished my mind could spark an image of life in this hollow
eternity...

I'LL BE DAMNED / '22

# THE MAILMAN

S teven turned the corner of Main and Elm. Wind gusted through the trees blowing debris along the empty streets. Steven looked into the candelit houses and saw shapes moving across blinds. He sorted the mail, dividing the Robinson's from the Martin's. As he sifted through the Franklin's parcels, an envelope corner slashed his thumb. Blood from the papercut dripped onto his blue-striped shorts.

He wrapped a rubber band tightly around the wound and licked a stamp, placing it over the cut. The sky turned dark. Power lines whipped through the wind. A sound of a distant train echoed through the alleyway.

*This day's never going to end*, Steven thought as he reflected on the hellish route.

First it was Clyde Roberts' smashing him in the face with his cane after his social security check didn't arrive. Steven took care of him in the usual way of whipping out his can of Mace and spraying. With Clyde incapacitated and the can of Mace safely tucked away, he had forgotten about Clyde's wife, Mildred, until she jumped from the roof and clubbed him over the head with her walker.

The old lady screamed and cursed at Steven over the social security check. Once the head lock was administered, she shut up as Steven raked his knuckles across her scalp.

**SHANE RYAN STALEY / 123**

"How you like that, lady?" Steven yelled, raking harder until her hairpiece flipped off.

Steven dragged the old lady over to a rose bush and shoved her backwards. Thorns shredded her pale, papery skin. He continued to drive her farther into the heart of the bush by pounding his mailbag atop her head.

As soon as she was totally silenced, Steven tossed the mailbag back over his shoulder and continued his route.

Steven shook his head, glad that the event was over.

The wind surged as raindrops pelted his bare arms and legs. A bolt of lightning streaked through a tree, hitting a mailbox across the road as the letters he had just delivered caught fire.

*Don't forget the motto*, Steven remembered. *Through rain, shine, snow or sleet, the mailman always delivers.*

"Probably even through a fucking tornado," Steven muttered to himself, watching a mass of black clouds swirling overhead.

Grabbing another bundle of mail, he noticed two new names on the block: Mr. Grimm and Mr. Beasley, who had just moved into neighboring houses.

Steven glanced at the shadowy house inhabited by Mr. Grimm. He pulled out a brown package addressed to the man and scanned the label to verify the proper street address.

*Funny*, Steven thought, *Why would Mr. Grimm get a package from his next door neighbor, Mr. Beasley?*

As he thought, he heard a strange ticking sound and smelled a funny mixture of gunpowder and manure.

Steven carefully balanced the box in his hand, inching his way up the stairs. He felt something shift and collide with the side of the box. Steven flinched, swallowing hard as the ticking grew louder. He swore the box felt warm.

Steven gently placed the box next to the door, rang the doorbell and slowly moved away.

"I didn't notice a thing," Steven said to himself, glancing back at the house. He exhaled a deep breath and walked to the next house where a chain link fence wrapped around a shadowy broken-down trailer. He glanced up at the mailbox onto a reflective sticker which read: *Harry Beasley.* He shifted his view to the left and read the sign: *BEWARE OF DOG!*

Looking around the house, Steven saw no food bowls or mailman-sized chew toys. His hands sweat and his heart pounded as he gripped the can of Mace.

He unlatched the fence door and entered, closing the door behind him. He aimed the Mace in front of him, ready for any sudden movements.

Suddenly to the side, he heard a barking sound, fading into the howling wind. Steven stopped dead in his tracks and listened, hearing a strange *mechanical* barking sound from somewhere in the bushes.

He bent over and pushed the bushes back to the sight of a wind-up toy dog yelping and wagging its tail.

Steven laughed. He knelt down admiring the wind-up toy. His breathing returned to normal.

*Finally someone with a sense of humor,* Steven thought.

Then he noticed the toy dog foaming at the mouth.

The little, mechanical dog lunged at Steven, knocking him backwards onto the sidewalk. Its overpowering strength pinned Steven there as it nipped at his arms and legs, finally latching onto his midsection. Steven screamed wildly, pulling at the toy dog. He could feel its warm plastic ribcage pulsating with excitement as it shook its head violently.

Steven pulled at its jaws, trying to free his manhood. He felt warm, sticky liquid drip from the dog's mouth. Pockets of sour breath drifted to his nose. A warm mass plopped onto his stomach while a stream of warm liquid sprayed against his face.

Steven pried the jaws open, then slammed the dog against the sidewalk. Its toy body bounced across the cement and a leg popped off.

Steven picked up the plastic leg, examining the network of plastic veins and exposed muscles coated with a clear blood-like excretion, spurting from the severed limb.

The three-legged plastic dog scurried across the sidewalk and lunged at Steven again.

Steven quickly shoved the leg into its jaws. The dog fell into the grass, chewing on its own appendage, stripping its plastic flesh.

Steven ran up the stairs, fumbling the envelope. After recovering it, he noticed the title of *Sorcerer* printed on the envelope after Mr. Beasley's name. He stuffed the envelope into the box and hurdled the chain-link fence.

On the other side, he inspected his privates. He pulled out the first aid kit and carefully disinfected the bloody region of teeth marks around his testicles. The wound burned as the cool misty spray fell upon his skin.

The tip of his penis stung, his shaft throbbing with excruciating pain. Doubling over, Steven quickly realized that he had once again misplaced his canister of Bactine with a can of Mace.

Even through his own sobs, Steven could faintly hear a man laughing from somewhere inside the house.

Steven waved his fist. "That wasn't very funny."

Steven looked at his watch and realized he was four and a half hours behind schedule. He opened the bag, finding it full of large bulk rate envelopes stamped with Ed McMahon's face.

Steven slammed his mailbag against the ground and noticed a man peeking out of the neighboring house. The tiny, almost midget-sized, man timidly scanned the porch and found the package Steven had placed next to his door.

The tiny man looked puzzled at the box, then shook it. A crackling noise suddenly echoed and smoke rolled from the box.

"Oh shit!" The tiny man shrieked.

The box exploded. Debris showered Steven with lawn furniture, glass and scraps of splintered wood. A severed dwarf-hand flew beside him. The digits on the disembodied hand still moved like a spider from the contracting muscles.

The sight chilled Steven as he stomped on the hand to stop its movement.

The storm suddenly shifted from a heavy downpour to hail.

After taking a couple golf ball-sized shots on the skull, Steven began kicking his bag down the endless road with houses dotting each side like some twisted connect-the-dot puzzle which Steven had to solve by walking to each house.

And suddenly he realized he would have to do this again tomorrow. And the next day. The mail would keep coming. Nobody could stop it. His job would never end, he would never feel the satisfaction of completing a job. By the time Steven returned to the Post Office, he knew another day's worth of mail would have already arrived and he would have to start all over again.

Steven laughed madly at the notion.

"I'm sick of being a messenger!" he screamed at the row of houses before him. "I'm sick of delivering this crap! It will never end. I can't take it anymore!"

Steven pulled out a revolver and fired a couple of random shots into the neighboring houses. He fired again, targeting several mailboxes in his way as he stomped through ash and soot and laughed hideously through the maze of streets leading back to the Post Office.

# THE RONNIE LETTERS

Sept. 1, 1998
Dear Samantha,
    I was just passing by the other night when I saw you in your house. I stood in your garden, squashing tomatoes like you squashed my heart. I watched you for a long time and noticed how your body glowed in the half-light of your bedroom. You probably don't remember me — I'm the guy who lit your cigarette at Stubby's bar the other night. Call me and we'll get together. My number's 555-6669. Talk to you soon!

Sincerely,
Ronnie

******

Sept. 7, 1998
Samantha-
    My letter must have got lost in the mail since you haven't phoned yet. So I delivered this one. I hope you find it on your couch. Call me: 555-6669.

—Ronnie

******

Sept. 10, 1998

Samantha:

Okay bitch, you think you're too good or something? Huh? Too busy? What the hell's the problem? You too consumed with all the guys coming over all the time? Is it the one with the Harley, the Mustang, or the Camaro that just so happened to blow up outside your house last night that keeps you from calling me? Anyway, despite you continually ignoring me, I thought I'd give you another chance. You know the number, so call.

Love,
Ronnie

******

Sept. 12, 1998

Dear Whore-

I got your cat, bitch! Snagged it from the garden last night. Damn thing kept purring against my leg. I took it home and held it close when I went to bed. I dreamed about you cuddling up to the little fluffy-haired thing every night (except last night, of course) and I felt closer to you. The damn thing even smelled like your perfume. I must have dreamed a little too hard because I woke up and found the poor bloated thing with its head flat and fur heavily slobbered on (sorry, I must have mistook it for my pillow). Had one hell of a wet dream though! You better call me. I got my eye on your gerbil cage. The long-haired one with the red eyes is next!

—Ronnie

******

Sept. 13, 1998

I warned you! So I shouldn't feel bad about putting the Mountain Dew in the gerbil's water bottle. I watched the poor little guy's body swell until he exploded against the glass. He wasn't even the thirsty one! The other one (I assume to be a female from the hot and heavy activity that had been going on in that cage for the last week) didn't even flinch. She just backed up against the glass as her insides started pouring out behind her. So you've officially ran out of pets for me to threaten....I guess if you don't call I'll have to start adding pets to your house. I hear rats, snakes and scorpions make fine house guests!

I'm sitting by the phone.

Love Ya,
Ronnie

\*\*\*\*\*\*

Sept. 14, 1998
Sammy-
I suppose you think you're funny: putting that rusty bear trap in the garden next to the tomatoes! You're going to pay for that one, honey!

—Ron

\*\*\*\*\*\*

Sept. 25, 1998
Dear Samantha,
Did you get my package in the mail today? Thought I'd give you a little piece to hold you over. That's right — the doctor's had to amputate it — you happy now? Notice the pretty green and yellow infection around my ankle — wonder how the hell that happened? Now you really owe me a date!

See you soon,
Ronnie

\*\*\*\*\*\*

Sept. 26, 1998
Samantha:
Cops came by asking questions. Seems they have been looking for me for a couple weeks now after tracing the number I gave you. I just told them that you are just some psycho-bitch making this all up because you're pissed off at me because I won't go out with you. Nice try. I'll be over tonight.

—Ronnie

\*\*\*\*\*\*

Sept. 28, 1998
Samantha-
So you moved! Pretty clever indeed. I went by your vacated house, saw the for-sale sign and almost gave up. But then I heard around town that you got a neighbor who's one hell of a guy! I would've never found you if you hadn't moved next door. Come on over to apartment number 13 and party with me!

Your New Neighbor,
Ronnie

P.S. Quit moving the medicine cabinet. Don't make me drill another hole, dammit!

\*\*\*\*\*\*

Oct. 1, 1998
Dear Samantha, my love:
New house — nice!!! I followed the moving truck (Quite a task — driving a stick shift with one leg!). You missing anything — perhaps an entire underwear drawer? Paid the moving guy $50 for all of them. I like the black, see-through pair the best — it's you!

—Ron

\*\*\*\*\*\*

Oct. 7, 1998
Samantha:
Where have you been?  Haven't seen you around lately.
Nice try, but that fake obituary in the newspaper didn't fool
me.  Suicide — come on!  You could've been more creative
than that.  I'm still waiting for that call.  I miss you!

Love,
Ronnie

\*\*\*\*\*\*

Oct. 8, 1998
Samantha-
Boy do I feel like an ass.  You really are dead!  I went to
your funeral — nice layout — beautiful viewing — and
irresistible panties you had on.  Where did you get those at?
Anyway, it was a great addition to my collection!  And I
finally got to touch you.  I met your parents, ate some cookies
— everything was wonderful.  I still haven't figured out how
you're going to receive this letter though.  Didn't leave me a
forwarding address — heaven or hell.  I'll find out.

—Ronnie

\*\*\*\*\*\*

Oct. 13, 1998
Samantha,
Can't mess with fate: we were always meant to be
together.  Pale and dirty, you still look beautiful.  But you
need to loosen up a little because the romance just isn't there.
So to fix the situation, I've contacted this guy I know.  He's
into the black magic / voodoo thing.  He put a spell on these
matching barbed-wire bracelets and explained to me that the
two people who wore them will be bound together in the
afterlife.  He assured me that it would work even if you had
already died.  I put the bracelet on your wrist and put the

I'LL BE DAMNED / 132

other one on mine. I know it will do the trick because the first night I wore the bracelet I dreamt about you screaming in this dark cavernous place as I tried to soothe your fear of the dark. I was with you all night, holding you and caressing the delicate curves of your body. I woke up fondling your corpse and became discouraged because I fell in love with your spirit as well as your body. So I went and bought a shot gun. I'm ready to eat a bullet for your true love so we can be together forever. I've tightened the bracelets and loaded the gun. Here I come, baby. The waiting is over...

Your Soul Mate,
Ronnie

# THE DAY MR. LANGFORD CRACKED

T hrough days of destruction and violence, it is common to only see demons and death and every other societal horror which cuts into the nerves as well as the soul, but Mr. Langford dreamed away from the mess of life, always remembering God's love and His eternity which awaited him. He looked to see pieces of heaven around him, vague little reminders of what was to come. But, even on the most blessed of all days, the symbols seemed to be fading.

Mr. Langford rose from bed and yawned. He shuffled to the window and glanced at the row of white, two-story houses which lined the roadway as far as he could see. *Such a beautiful world*, he thought, *such a lovely time to be alive!*

He descended the stairs and whispered "Good morning" to his wife nestled on the couch. He looked over at his brother, drunk and naked beside her. He shook his head. *It's not love, so it doesn't matter.*

After inhaling a bagel, he grabbed his briefcase and headed out the door. To the side of the house, he scanned the empty space, envisioning a giant pool. As his mind drifted, he saw his children on a hot summer day splashing and diving into cool blue waters as his wife's shapely body lay across the patio sporting that yellow two-piece. He smiled, took a deep breath and realized this could be the day he finally got that bonus. And the pool could be just weeks away.

The morning commute to work was a refreshing time for Mr. Langford. He cherished the dawn, the fresh morning air preparing him for the day ahead. But after a block of road construction, three detours and a mile long traffic jam, he pulled into the parking garage, feeling bitterly distressed. It wasn't just the old lady who had flipped him off in rush hour traffic, but the entire mood of everyone on the highway. Horns blared, gun shots echoed following waves of shouting and cursing. It almost seemed as if there was some mad virus carried by the wind, infecting everyone on the road.

Mr. Langford tried to shake the recollection from his mind. He looked away to the blue skies and watched birds glide gracefully overhead. A sudden tranquility swept over him, his body relaxed.

Mr. Carlson greeted him at the door to his office.

"You're late, Langford, do I have to start making you punch a time clock?"

Mr. Langford smiled. "I will amend my morning schedule to leave a half-hour early, sir."

"Fine," Carlson said, "Do whatever it takes because I went over your advertising campaign and it stinks."

"Yes sir," Mr. Langford nodded, "I'd love to revise it immediately."

Carlson winced. "And while I'm here, I'll save you a trip to my office by letting you know that I gave the promotion to Johnson and the company plans to downsize which means no bonus and everyone will have to take a fifteen percent pay cut."

"But—"

"Any questions? No? Good!"

Mr. Langford sat down, stunned and disheartened. Throughout the morning hours, he stayed at his desk, staring at a blank sheet of paper, his creative outlet clogged.

Bernice, the secretary, poked her head into his cubicle. "Here's your lunch, Mr. Langford. And I have some messages for you."

"Oh, thank you, Bernice," he said, smiling. "You look very lovely today."

Bernice blushed while reading off his messages: "Bookman called and he hates your sales pitch, the dry cleaners called and said they ruined your new suit, your mother called and said that your father had passed away, your neighbor called and said that your wife ran off with your brother and left the kids home alone, and the fire department called and said that your kids have set fire to your house."

"Is that all?"

Bernice flipped through her papers. "Oh," she said suddenly, "I almost forgot about the man who called and said something about one of your stocks crashing."

"Okay, thank you. Can you please tell Mr. Carlson that I'll be leaving early."

A bead of sweat rolled down Mr. Langford's cheek. His mind spun, his eyelid twitched. *Deep breath. Slow, deep breath.*

He closed his eyes and exhaled. Reopening them, he focused on Mr. Carlson hovering over him, his face fiery red.

"You're fired, Langford. Pack up your things and get the hell out of my office!"

Three steps out into the parking garage, Mr. Langford noticed an older gentleman in a blue suit pacing in front of his car. Suddenly he remembered the gas line leak he had neglected to get repaired as the man flicked his cigarette on the pavement.

A trail of fire worked its way under the car. Mr. Langford watched the fiery ball expand as his car exploded. He quickly ducked as the older gentleman's body blew past him, bouncing off a concrete support beam. Shrapnel from the blast veered off other cars, cracking windshields, denting frames and chipping paint. His car's antenna shot out, piercing him in the ass. Mr. Langford quickly dropped his belongings, and pulled the wiry piece out. He suddenly felt a strange sense of numbness spreading from his bloody cheek to his emotions. He felt oddly cold.

The day had gone from bad to worse. His regular monotonous schedule, which rarely yielded any such deviations from the norm, had turned horribly different and he found himself fearing the unknown. He was no longer comfortably at ease with himself nor anything around him as a restless discontent threatened to surface. He fought off the coming mood, trying to forget about the day's trials and focus onto better things.

But the odd feeling persisted as he trudged through the crowded street on his way home. He looked toward the sky to refresh himself, but could only see the mammoth stone buildings bobbing in an ocean of asphalt. The towers loomed over him, shadowing sunlight. Exhaust from cars drifted, stinging his nose. People on the sidewalk ran into him, shoving him aside.

"It is a gift to be one of the living, to be one of God's children living in His glorious creation," he recited. A surge of energy rejuvenated him, a smile slid across his face.

Passing the business district, he walked several blocks to a side street filled with houses with white picket fences. He looked to the sky and saw white cumulus clouds speckling blue skies.

*Tomorrow will be a better day*, he thought, rejoicing, *Just draw from the good each day has to offer and look forward to the next.*

He held his head high and walked steadily until a tiny dog hurdled a nearby fence and latched onto his crotch. Pain jolted through his midsection as the dog tugged and shook its head wildly, tearing his pants. Mr. Langford managed to pry its jaws from his manhood and toss it aside. The dog slid on the sidewalk and scampered toward him for another attack.

Without a thought, Mr. Langford punted the miniature dog back over the fence. The dog flailed helplessly through the air until it smacked the side of the house and fell limply to the ground.

"Oh my God, what have I done?"

Mr. Langford quickly walked away from the scene.

Dazed, he continued staring at the sky while asking God to forgive his actions. He prayed for God to mend the day and make it better.

Up ahead, he watched two young boys with a beebee gun, aiming at birds on a power line.

"Stop!" Mr. Langford yelled, approaching the children. He finally felt that God had answered his prayer, giving him a chance at retribution. "Animals are our friends." He looked directly above him and pointed to several birds on the line. He wanted to convince them not to harm the birds, knowing one day they would regret their ignorant actions. "Birds are God's creation, like yourself, and should be allowed to share this wonderful planet."

The two boys looked strangely at one another and shook their heads.

As Mr. Langford continued his speech, he felt the gentle splatter of bird droppings atop his bald spot.

The boys broke down in laughter. They quickly doubled over, holding their stomachs, as their faces turned red.

Mr. Langford felt the stream of bird crap run down his face. He felt massive pressure building in his head, his face burned. His mind went blank, his feelings numbed. A smile washed over his face, but it wasn't a grin of happiness this time.

He grabbed the beebee gun and fired, picking off a bird on the line. He pumped the gun again and fired aimlessly.

Now wide-eyed and serious, the boys stumbled back, gasping in horror.

Feathers floated from the line as the birds scattered. Mr. Langford pumped the gun again and again, taking down birds in flight. Soon the chamber was empty as the two boys stared silently, watching a madman laughing hideously while peering down at the bodies of six bloody chickadees strewn across the lawn.

Mr. Langford handed the gun back to one of the boys and walked onward, finally reaching the smoldering remains of his house. The kids were chasing one another in the yard as a few firemen and observers trudged through the ashes.

Mr. Langford felt the hideous grin grow wider as he located the side plot of land and envisioned the pool filled with dead chickadees and his wife's bloated body.

"Hey kids," he yelled, watching them stop and stare. "Remember that pool I promised you?"

His son and daughter smiled, jumping up and down.

Mr. Langford's smile peaked as he fell to his knees, digging wildly with his hands. Six hours later, he rose, turned on the hose and began filling the giant hole he had created.

Slowly, before the dirt hole was completely full, he watched a skeleton float to the surface.

His son gasped, "Spot?"

His daughter screamed.

It had been less than a year since Mr. Langford had buried the family dog there, but it was well-stripped of muscle and flesh. As he shook it, its shriveled brain rattled inside its skull.

Mr. Langford yanked the canine's skeleton from the mud hole. He studied its structure and laughed at the simplicity in which a living thing had transformed into a decayed set of bones.

Suddenly everything seemed meaningless, the entire world a lost place for temporary travelers on route to their ultimate demise. As he looked back at his children, they seemed but mere strangers staring coldly back at him.

His neighbor poked his head from the bushes. "Good afternoon, Mr. Langford."

"What's so fucking *good* about it?" Mr. Langford shouted, "Go *fuck* yourself!"

The neighbor's eyes flashed with surprise, shock, then total disgust and contempt.

Somebody suddenly touched Mr. Langford on the shoulder. He whirled around to face two men he quickly recognized as Jehovah's Witnesses.

"Do you have a few minutes for us to come into your home and discuss spiritual issues with you and your family?" a skinny, bald-headed man said, glancing sporadically at the burnt, half-collapsed house behind him.

Mr. Langford punched him in the face, grabbed him by the collar and flung him into the pool. The other man ran away, dropping an armful of pamphlets which blew across the yard.

Mr. Langford felt a steady rumbling of laughter escape his mouth. He looked up to the sky, raised his hand and extended his middle finger. "Hey God, why don't you get *your* ass down here and do this for a change, you big pussy!!!"

Mr. Langford's fists clinched up in rage as he suddenly felt something pop in his head. The vision in his right eye went black.

Sirens wailed down the street. His children bawled. Tires screeched.

Mr. Langford looked around with his left eye, taking in the ruined house, the Jehovah's Witness floating in the murky depths of his new pool, the dog skeleton, the now overcast sky and all the God-damn birds flying overhead.

He wanted a gun, a weapon to annihilate the entire world, just not one lousy bird or human at a time. He wanted a weapon so powerful and far ranging that it could vaporize the entire God-forsaken planet with one pull on the trigger.

But he would never get the chance. Bound to the handcuffs and shackles, an officer slipped the straitjacket over his head and tightened it. A man with a stretcher stopped next to him, loading him in an ambulance. As the vision blurred in his only remaining eye, he could barely make out the reflective sticker plastered on the side: HARGROVE MENTAL WARD.

Mr. Langford closed his eyes, feeling his body rock back

and forth. Faster and faster, his only thought was of the cool waters of the pool and how he longed to dive into the muddy mess and never return.

He drifted off to the vision of blue skies and slack-necked chickadees. His face cramped with laughter, his jaw aching from the smile permanently etched onto his sagging face.

Mr. Langford had never felt more alive or alone as the van spiraled down an exit ramp, circling in descent, lower and lower, around and around, the scenery swirling under grey skies, deeper into darkness, downward toward the unknown.

# THE GOLDEN YEARS

Cameron glanced into the dark hallway with shadowy shapes lumbering up and down the strip. Sweat beaded on his forehead as he watched two old men wrestling in their pajamas, their bony arms and legs flailing against each others in an apparent disagreement over a bingo prize. Suddenly someone grabbed his ass from behind.

Cameron turned around to an old woman in a wheelchair licking her cracked lips. He slowly backed his way through the doorway to his aunt's room and shut the door behind him.

Cameron hated nursing homes. Besides the rotten smell of old life withering away, there were the old men cutting farts in the hallway and old women walking around without pants and dentures. He dared not venture into the cafeteria and listen to all the mouths chewing, joints clicking away, lips sucking on applesauce and air, droplets of liquefied beef dripping onto meal-splattered tables and symphonies of low- and high-pitched flatulence echoing through plastic chairs. Whenever he visited Aunt Betty, he stayed in her room, only leaving to use the restroom and to exit the cursed place.

"Sir, I thought I told you to please step outside?" the nurse said, adjusting a pair of rubber gloves while holding a bed pan. Aunt Betty's usual hollow stare erupted with a wide grin after noticing her hind quarter had been freed from the soiled linen and cold plastic make-shift toilet.

The nurse stared at Cameron as he slowly opened the door, peeking outside. His heart pounded harder, sweat rolling from his forehead. He took a deep breath, seeing no one abroad, and slipped carefully out the doorway.

Dark rooms filled with television and rag-time music lined the hallway as Cameron kept a watchful eye for slippered feet or rubber wheels peeking from any of the rooms. Old Mrs. Witherspoon's room was two doors down. He always avoided crossing that room because every time he did, she saw him and screamed "A fuck for a buck, young man." Before Cameron could flee, she would drop off the bed and pull herself across the tiled floor, dragging her one-legged body out into the hallway in hot pursuit.

Cameron shivered thinking about the horrible old woman and so he walked in the other direction and soon found a bench alongside the lobby wall. Cameron crossed his legs and waited for the nurse to finish.

*This will be the last week I visit*, he thought. He dreaded coming here each week, but felt as if he was obligated since most of his aunt's immediate family had moved out west. Plus, he was in her will. He didn't want a healthy claim to real estate, as well as the generous cash offering, to change hands to some poor orderly who paid more attention.

An old lady shuffled in front of him and smiled. Cameron looked the other direction, pretending not to notice her.

"May I sit with you?" she asked.

Cameron hesitated, then nodded.

The old lady maneuvered her rickety bones against the wooden bench and sighed. Her white hair was neatly trimmed and styled, except for the row of curlers still matted and tangled toward the back.

"My feet are killing me," she said, taking off her pink, fuzzy slippers.

Cameron glanced down at the layer of dead skin on her foot. His body tensed to the sight as she scratched her heel, raking off the top layer. As the skin fell to the floor, Cameron noticed the interlocking, razor-sharp parting line which seemed to separate her heel from the arc in her foot.

Cameron looked closer realizing that the line shifted like something was moving inside, the pointed, dried up blades of skin seeming to be flexing like a set of chewing teeth.

*My feet are killing me.* The whole phrase took on a horrific new meaning as the fissure gapped wider. Cameron saw a sort of cavity emerge deep inside, funneling into her leg. Strings of fluid stretched with the gaping void. A long, narrow tongue-like projection flailed just inside the flesh.

Suddenly her leg contorted upward, cartilage snapping as it was guided by the foot, until it hooked across her shoulder. A sick chill coursed though Cameron's body as the tongue-like extension rolled from within the cavity, desperately stretching toward the old woman's neck.

The old woman grunted as she pushed her leg back down and held it there, her arm quivering violently. Her foot stomped, smashing the extended fleshy projection against the floor. A piercing animalistic squeal sounded from inside the woman as the mashed secondary appendage retracted into her body.

Cameron, recovering from shock, managed to finally pull his attention away from the foot. He prepared himself to run away, but feared that in his retreat, the tongue-thing hiding inside her foot would lash out and coil around his neck or burrow into his body.

The thought alone panicked him as he lunged off the bench and sprinted toward his aunt's room.

Luckily, the door was opening as the nurse exited.

Cameron, out of breath, ducked into the dark room and slammed the door shut, pinning his body against the frame. Aunt Betty just smiled at him as he fumbled around in his pockets in search of his lighter.

"God, I need a smoke," Cameron said, pulling out the pack. He popped a cigarette in his mouth and flicked the lighter.

Aunt Betty frowned. "You know that's bad for your

health, dear. Those things will kill you before you're fifty!"

A sinister smile washed over Cameron's face. "Good," he said, "That's very good!" Cameron laughed hideously, pulling another cigarette from his shirt pocket and popping that one in his mouth along with the other one. He sparked the lighter and puffed wildly on both of them.

"Cameron, dear," Aunt Betty said, shaking her head. "If you won't stop for yourself, please do it for me. My lungs are killing me."

Cameron's mouth flew open, the cigarettes dropping to the floor, as his aunt retched, the withered skin around her mouth expanding to where tiny white stretch marks appeared like worms just beneath the skin. As she coughed, thin rope-like strands of organ tissues wavered from deep within her throat. The wet grey noodle-like extensions lashed into mid-air, eclipsing her face.

She quickly cleared her throat, calming the fluctuation while using her bony fingers to push the now limp projectiles back down into her esophagus. She took a deep breath as Cameron could hear the thin strands being sucked back into her body.

"Would you care for some tea?" she asked, her glassy eyes scanning him.

Cameron swallowed hard, staring down at the expanding patch of carpet smoldering beneath the tip of his cigarettes. He lifted his foot to stomp the cigarette out, but then hesitated. He removed his foot from hovering over the singed carpet, ushering in more oxygen to the site.

Cameron smiled after the flames appeared. He stepped out into the hallway, shut the door behind him and strolled out through the exit into the aging world beyond. The distant neon lights of a liquor store caught his attention as he felt his shirt pocket, making sure his pack of cigarettes were still there.

Tonight he would drink and smoke like there was no tomorrow.

# NATURAL SELECTION

As a child, I was fascinated with the order of living things and how we evolved into a civilization of humans sharing this strange planet with animals and insects. My father had once told me a story about evolving out of primordial soup and I had always envisioned God squeezing one off into this murky medium-sized mud hole which later transformed into the big mess called life.

And throughout my childhood days, I spent long hours observing nature: grasshoppers in the alleyway, bumblebees in the garden, and my neighbor Erica's beautifully shaped breasts blossoming before anyone else her age.

Nature was a real trip. The whole cycle intrigued me; how each day a special task was assigned to each living thing which, in turn, gave back a little something to the earth. Like a simple chain such as sunlight fulfilling millions of plants and trees which provided oxygen and food and shelter for insects and animals and humans. And as insects and animals both played a part in the cycle of earth and existence, humans merely sucked the life out of it.

It's a wonder why many think we're such a dominant species on this planet. But early on, I found out that nature was just humoring us by letting us think we had some sort of control.

One afternoon, I remember stumbling onto a strange

little insect with beady black orbs and oversized antenna. The thing freaked me out. I had never seen such a bug before — it seemed to move its body with mine, to where it was always facing me as if it expected me to attack at any moment. It moved quickly in the residue of my shadow, cramming its winged quarters beneath an exposed root of the big dead elm in the back yard. I hunched over it and flicked it with a stick until it was squirming on its back. And in the flurry of twitches, I witnessed the deep green oval on its underside.

"Stink Bug!" my friend Shawn yelled from behind, scaring the living hell out of me.

I took a few steps back, watching the bug regain its stance, reinstating its beady-eyed glare.

Shawn set his sights on my point of focus. I looked over at him as he suddenly clutched his chest like I had just uncovered a nest of rattle snakes or a hidden den of demons in my own back yard.

Being the daring one, I reached down and cupped my hand over the bug, scooping its stick-frame in one hand.

"God-damn, put that thing down!" he yelled, taking a few additional steps back.

I lifted the bug to my nose and took a whiff. The vague smell of dirt and bug matter wafted toward me.

"It doesn't stink at all," I replied, looking somewhat puzzled.

Shawn rolled his eyes and shook his head. "It doesn't stink unless you squish it, stupid."

He must have seen my eyes light up because he literally screamed, "Don't you dare — are you nuts?"

I shook my head and laughed, shoving the bug toward him.

"It's just a little bug, what are you so freaked out about?"

Shawn swallowed hard. "That is the green-spotted stink bug — those things are bad news — a ton more powerful than the average stink bug!"

"Bull shit — you're so full of it," I said, pinching the end of the insect until a green discharge squirted on his pants. Suddenly the smell hit me. God, the most pungent of smells couldn't even be classified in the same rank. I peered down at Shawn's jeans and watched his face turn bright red. The stink rose and swirled around us. My vision blackened. I stumbled back, trying to shake the sickly feel of liquid insect guts from my index finger and thumb. I wiped my hand on the grass. The smell of freshly cut lawn and the God-awful stench struck me head-on. My eyes watered, drying in their sockets. I felt a stream of snot pour from my nose.

Through blurred vision, I watched Shawn vomit onto his pant leg. He shook uncontrollably, like a rabid mole or psychotic earthworm trying to burrow into cement.

Meanwhile I felt paralyzed, trapped in the draught of sour air. As I peered at the tainted hand, I noticed I had unconsciously rubbed several layers of skin from my thumb. Blood oozed from the joint.

Glancing around the neighborhood, I realized how far the smell had traveled because three houses down Mr. Baker cursed, violently fanning his nose while falling off his rooftop and landing atop a car. A flock of pigeons hit the stink zone, several plummeting from the sky, bouncing off the pavement. A stray cat fluffed out its fur and hissed wildly, spinning itself around in the alleyway.

A hot summer breeze erupted, momentarily bringing in a much needed relief. I looked over at Shawn whose head was almost completely buried in topsoil where a handful of stink bugs swarmed through a channel to a deep dark opening, a nest where I imagined an entire colony of the strange insects wriggled atop one another.

I looked around and took note of the mutated scenery. Trees had withered, leaves already fallen in mid-summer. Flowers now slumped, anchored to dried and lifeless roots. Windows were already boarded up. Dead birds littered lawns and streets. Animals stumbled, vacant-eyed and twitching madly, as if hit by cars. I even spotted a few distant neighbors passed out on porches, apparently overcome by the fierce stench.

The world moved in slow-motion, dazed at the mid-afternoon event. As I returned to the dreaded spot, I saw something out of the corner of my eye. The beady eyes and twiggy legs scurrying beneath the shed.

A flurry of ideas struck me and I smiled, quickly grabbing an old dust pan in the shed. I peered beneath the foundation with the jar ready and scraped beneath, hoping to God I could catch the thing without smashing it.

******

Fridays were always reserved for feeding Petey. The sixth grade's pet toad possessed a weird gaze as I tossed the bug into the cage. The offering quickly mounted the toad, making its way up to his head. The toad blinked one eye and cocked his head, finally showing some interest.

This was my cue to get the hell out of there.

I asked Mrs. Waters if I could use the restroom and when she nodded, I quickly exited.

I peered around the corner and watched the aquarium as Petey flicked the bug off and positioned himself within striking distance. The class crowded closer to the tank.

"Ah cool, he's gettin' ready to eat him," somebody whispered.

In a flurry of motion, poor Petey coiled his tongue around the bug and reeled it in.

First there was some violent jaw movement, then a shudder and a mad hop, followed by dark eyes bulging from their sockets and a sticky-dry tongue expelled onto the glass. From there it got a little hazy as classmates shifted in front of my view, but what I did see was a wildly flailing toad with green liquid spurting from its mouth and nose. Its throat swelled and contracted, then swelled bigger until a spray of blood painted the glass.

There was a chorus of screams and a violent shuffle of

girls and boys trampling one another in attempts to move away, but it was too late for Erica.

The toad was thrashing around so violently it broke through the screen and stuck on Erica's chest, right between her cleavage, and kicked wildly, tongue flickering through the air. Its actions seemed almost unreal for such a creature to commit, but it soon ended as the toad's violent thrashing turned to a lesser tick of the head, then a dead, hollow-sounding thud onto the floor.

The first wave of the incredible aroma began to spread its way down the hallway as I sprinted down the stairs.

******

The little episode at school cost me three days suspension. A few days later, during my time off, I went digging and uncovered the entire nest of stink bugs. In the middle, I collected the mother of all stink bugs — a queen I would guess. Its bulbous hind quarters are filled with a quaint red liquid which you can visibly see within its translucent body. Its giant rear end had to be the size of a quarter.

Since I captured it in the Mason jar, its size has almost tripled, red fluids swirling angrily whenever I tap on the glass. But the weirdest thing of all is that I'm twenty-five now and the thing's still alive. Without food or water, it has survived all these years in the jar. It frantically claws at the base of the glass, its red beady eyes luring me to release it and pinch its oversized ass.

Last night, I dreamt of Erica naked on the floor. After all the years of secretly watching her from afar, I was rubbing her enormous breasts as she squirmed atop me. She rocked wildly and I squeezed harder until she finally climaxed. As I opened my eyes, I noticed I had punctured both breasts. Green and red fluids trickled down her stomach and on to my legs, burning my skin as I held my breath against the stinging smell of her release.

I awoke screaming. A stream of moonlight fell across my room enlightening the jar where the strange insect stared. I grabbed the jar and returned to bed, gazing at the swirling fluids inside. Its red eyes glared at me and images raced in my mind, as if transmitted from its own thoughts. I felt danger in watching the insect, like I had enveloped a tiny virus or atomic bomb in a jar. I swear it has existed all these years, created as the earth's own defense mechanism toward ridding itself from its most harmful parasite.

Knowing this, I get the insane urge to take it to a Garth Brooks concert and let it loose beneath a thousand cowboy boots stomping to their final beat. Or possibly attend church for the first time, accompanied with an offering the congregation will never forget.

But then there is a stronger urge to wait until New Year's Eve and watch the ball drop in Times Square. And when the champagne bottles pop, so will the bug. And the eve of the new year will become the eve of destruction.

Which doesn't give me much time to finally get into Erica's pants for real.

# OPPORTUNITIES

M oney makes the world go around. You can buy anything with it: love, sex and death, and I make a living off the latter.

Killing people on contract isn't what it used to be. But the most important thing is that the pay's good, even though the stress will kill you in the end, if nothing else does. I didn't choose the job, the job chose me. I'd been a natural ever since I was eight years old, standing in front of my lemonade stand while I tried to teach my brother the importance of making money. It was all due to *opportunity,* I told him. But he would never listen. Even up until today, he is jobless and still lives with my parents in Indiana.

I had set up the stand during the very last day of summer in 1984. The weather was cooling, the day life had seemed to slow almost overnight. It was a strange time to sell lemonade and to make a profit doing so, but I had insisted on showing James how far a dollar could be stretched with the right brains behind the idea.

I had mixed the lemonade in the garage using various oils and jugs of antifreeze, along with some household chemicals while squeezing fresh lemons into the mixture to block out the quaint smell.

A neighbor's cat had wandered by to be the first test subject. In a small saucer, I had mixed the concoction with milk. The cat lapped the saucer dry. It slowly stumbled next to a trash can, its tail whipping around, its fur puffed out madly. I watched in amazement as the cat hissed in our direction, fell over a few times, then scampered into the side of the house. I watched the feline sprawled on its back, a tiny fountain of blood and fluid spurting from its gasping mouth. It flopped onto its side, then onto all fours as it streaked across the yard in our direction.

James lunged atop the lemonade stand and I ran into the street as the damn thing jumped onto my pant legs, its claws digging into my skin furiously. I peered into its wicked yellow eyes and saw a weakness, a hint of helplessness and fear. And I felt a sense of purpose, of fulfillment, as I watched its last moments unveil directly before my eyes.

Another spray of blood erupted from its mouth. It gagged, craning its neck, like it had been trying to expel some mammoth hairball. I took it by the throat and tossed it into the street.

Three consecutive cars took out its legs, back, and remainder of any skull it possessed. It twitched there in front of our lemonade stand until our first customer wandered by.

"Hello, kids," the older gentleman greeted us with a smile. His blue suit and matching tie caught my eye right away. Dad was just a factory man, barely making ends meet, barely holding the family together, and I never wanted to be like that. I wanted to be wearing a suit and tie, a genuine marker of my success, as this guy was.

The man cringed, checking out the smashed roadkill just a few feet from our stand. Flies began to buzz around its carcass as an occasional shudder spilled forth from its hind quarters.

He chucked a quarter at James and I handed him a cup, attempting to conceal my widening grin. He sniffed the rim and I thought we were out of business, but then he saluted us, tipping the cup our way, then downed the entire drink.

I had never seen a grown man bawl like a little child before. Red-eyed and snotty-nosed, he crawled along the curbside, holding his stomach. Unlike the cat, he never vomited once. Instead, he just shook and cursed a lot, dragging his briefcase along for the ride, as if he was going to need it later.

Several cars passed with uncaring gazes, even after seeing a grown man in a suit crawling along the roadside. By the time the guy finally collapsed, I went through his briefcase and wallet, pulled out a money clip full of hundred dollar bills.

"You see," I lectured, "This is how you really cash in on opportunity and take a job to its next level."

We had started with a measly quarter, and had advanced to over five hundred dollars in just a few minutes. And we weren't finished yet...

We pulled him by his tie through a series of back yards until it snapped off, then each grabbed a leg and continued. While cutting through one yard, a pit bull broke its chain and jumped atop the guy's corpse. At first it clamped down on the guy's forearm. Then it backed off and straddled him, pumping its midsection into the guy's behind. And some sort of strange expression had settled onto the guy's face, like he had almost enjoyed it.

Man, I had never laughed so hard in my life! Both James and I were hunched over, gasping for air, trying not to look at this most ridiculous sight. I turned to James and said jokingly, "What's the matter honey...bad day at the office?"

Finally we managed to pull the corpse away from the dog and drag it across a couple more yards to Mr. Reynolds'.

Mr. Reynolds was queer as they come. Looked kinda like a Mr. Rogers-type but with a taste for flesh. And we had some fresh meat to deliver.

Another couple hundred dollars and we closed shop for the day.

Memories are strange sometimes. They come and go and each time they do, they seem to get further away.

Anyway, I took to killing for money. Business is booming. And everything was going smoothly, until Dad called me a few days back and had a job for me. He had cashed in his entire 401K just to take out my mother. He said if I didn't do it, then James would surely take the money and close the deal in a heartbeat.

But I was always Dad's favorite. So he gave me the first opportunity.

The job proposed some big concerns. My ultimate advantage to being an assassin was anonymity. But now, I found myself strolling into downtown, Whisper Ridge, returning some 20 years after I had first left to whack my mother.

Christ! I ran into an old friend at the gas station and one of my old high school teachers at the McMurtry's Gun Shoppe. Old man McMurtry asked how my parents were doing. He also informed me that Dad had been laid off for almost six months now as the factory had closed. Dad had never mentioned it on the phone.

I arrived at the house around noon and Mom was sweeping the house. Dad was out fishing somewhere. After a hug and a kiss, she slid me an envelope full of hundreds and said, "Here. I want that bastard dead by sunset."

I looked at her strange and sifted through the money.

"After your grandfather died, I had inherited quite a bit of money which I left in savings," she continued. "It's yours if you'll take care of him. And make it neat, like he ran off. I don't want his body to even wash ashore."

An interesting scenario. Now I could've whacked Mom, then waited for Dad to get off work and take care of him as well, but then the guilt might set in. What would Mother think in her final few moments when I took her money and killed her instead. I wanted to be fair about the whole thing, and when she invited me back for supper later, I agreed. They'd both be there. I'd just present them the money, acknowledge both their offerings, make my final apologies and end the deal the easiest of ways.

\*\*\*\*\*\*

SHANE RYAN STALEY / 155

Dad was quiet throughout supper, a bead of sweat had formed on his forehead, glistening in the ray off the overhead light. Mom just smiled and made small talk. James even showed up to bum some more food off them. He still technically lived there – at age 28 – and Mom obviously hated him for it. She had mentioned it during our earlier meeting, but neglected to go into detail about his irresponsibility and how he had sucked them dry over the years, both financially and emotionally.

I felt like pulling him into another room and letting him know what was going on, but I thought it might be too suspicious. So I just finished my supper and quietly maneuvered to the kitchen.

"How about I make some lemonade," I said, winking at my brother. "Would you mind helping me, James?"

James flashed a guilty, concerned look in my direction, then wiped his face clean and met me in the kitchen.

"What the hell are you doing, are you nuts?" he whispered.

"They both paid me to kill the other one!"

James shook his head, confused. His eyes suddenly grew large. "I think we better get the fuck out of here!"

"Why?"

"It's a setup," he explained. "Something's screwy! They've been acting weird all week, been whispering around me, been eyeballing me."

"It doesn't make sense."

"Sure it does," James said, looking over his shoulder. "Do you think it was just some strange coincidence that they invited you here after 15 years and both secretly offered you money to knock off the other?"

"Stranger things have happened," I replied, remembering one hit I was paid to do in Ohio. I was in the process of driving into this small town to knock off a guy named Leon Finckley who was actually a rival hitman. The ironic part was that some rich husband had hired me after finding out his wife had hired Finckley to knock him off. The man paid me to do Finckley first, then his wife next before she would hire a replacement killer.

I had been nervous for days about that hit, knowing I was in for a real challenge. As I drove to his hometown, I pulled over for a man who had a flat tire on a barren stretch of road just miles outside of town. I didn't stop to help the man out as much as I did to ask some questions about this Leon-character. I was quite pleased when the man extended his hand and said, "I'm Leon Finckley. Are you looking for a job that needs done?"

His smug little grin was wiped off instantly by the sound of a bullet ripping through his brain. I stuffed his body in the trunk with the jack and drove away with a hundred grand in a matter of minutes. If only everything went that smoothly...

I thought about the situation and I, too, began to feel paranoid. They knew the only way I would come back to Whisper Ridge was on business, so maybe there was an ulterior motive. They were testing me for something, but what?

"I got a bad feeling," James said. Sweat started to accumulate on his forehead.

I thought I knew what he meant until he dropped to his knees and fell face first into the hardwood floor. I turned him over to a terrible gurgling sound, a sputter of escaped breath, then nothing.

It had to be something planted in the food.

Everything seemed to be coming in on me at once, like the whole town was just a prop with characters and plots sent to seduce me to my ultimate demise.

I pulled my gun out, entered the dining room and found the room empty. I grabbed my jacket and found that both envelopes had been taken from my pockets. In their place was a note that read: *Now it's my turn.* The handwritten note was signed *Leon Finckley.*

The fucker was still alive. I was so sure he was a goner, left for dead inside a trunk on a lonely country road in midsummer heat.

Now he had obviously sought revenge and had paid off my very own parents. Dad had lied about the 401K money and Mom about the inheritance. I should've known they were both still penniless, like they had always been with Dad in a factory, now jobless, and Mom working at home. How was I so blind?

I searched the entire house from the attic to the basement and found no traces of either Mother or Father. I tore through their files looking for money to burn as my stomach suddenly cramped. A funny taste settled in the back of my throat.

In searching, I found an extra life insurance policy taken out on James and dated just a month prior to my visit.

I managed to make it to a nearby hotel before my bowels gave way to blood and poison. I don't know why the poison finished James off so quickly and has taken its time on me, but my body has turned numb in places and I can't type much longer. I wanted to get this all down before the poison runs its course. I wanted it to be a last confession before I die and also to serve as evidence in my murder. Maybe someone will find it and make light on my traitor parents, so they won't be able to squander the cash that Leon had paid them, nor cash in on my brother's life insurance policy.

I pray for a maid to collect the evidence, but that hope is dimming to a shadow of a man in the motel's window. He is sitting in a wheelchair with a smug little grin, laughing from time to time, as he waits outside for the opportunity to revel in his revenge...

# THE BECOMING

Mikila brushed her hair from her eyes and pulled her T-shirt over her head. Her boyfriend, Jeff, slammed the bedroom door and stomped down the stairs. She listened for the sound of his truck peeling across the driveway, but, instead, shouts of anger echoed closer along with footsteps running back up the stairs.

"Damn you Mikila," Jeff shouted, slamming the door against the wall, "We can't afford to raise this child. I'm not giving up my life for a little piss-ant running around the house, sponging off us for eighteen fucking years!"

"It's not my fucking fault! It takes two to get pregnant, you dumb *shit!*"

Jeff slapped her across the face and threw her onto the couch. He grabbed his crotch and thrust his hips in her direction. "If you didn't always want *this* so bad, you wouldn't have gotten knocked up!"

"Fuck you!" she screamed. "If you weren't always so drunk, you would've worn protection instead of raping me, you worthless piece of shit."

"We're aborting this baby – I'm not paying you child support – it was your mistake, not mine!"

"Go to hell!" Mikila spat. "I'm having this child whether you like it or not."

"Oh yeah!" Jeff said, drawing closer. In a flurry of

movement, he suddenly lurched at her, his fist barreling into her stomach. Mikila stumbled back, her vision flickering as the pain shot through her entire body.

\*\*\*\*\*\*

An hour later Mikila regained consciousness to a pounding, cramping pain in her right side. Through the picture window, she saw that Jeff's truck was gone. Darkness enveloped the entire house. Her head spun as she rose, stumbling toward the bathroom. Once there, she sat on the toilet, relieving her achy bladder.

She stared into her pale reflection on the full-sized mirror and noticed Jeff's handprint still etched on her face. The smell of alcohol and his cologne still lingered in the musty apartment. She watched the tears stream down her face as hatred slowly began to resurface.

The stream of urine suddenly stopped to a burning sensation that quickly turned to excruciating pain. Her stomach contracted and something splattered inside the bowl as she felt a warm mass escape her.

She felt the mass continue to slip past her clenched legs and splash into the toilet. The feeling and sound made her instantly gag, a stream of vomit following, splashing the linoleum.

Mikila glanced beneath her at the ripples of bloody water swirling toward the bottom. Strands of pale flesh spiraled up the bowl's side, desperately clinging to the porcelain.

In the middle of the bowl, there appeared a tiny mass, almost like a portion of an organ, a liver perhaps. It maneuvered like a fish at first, then floated down into the darkness of the toilet's piping.

Panic suddenly gripped her, her heart racing, legs quivering against the cold porcelain. "Oh my God, no!"

She knelt and swept her hand into the clouded water, fishing for what had disappeared. Fear swept over her. Adrenaline rushed through her veins. She felt the fleshy strips curl around her wrist, caressing her, binding her, urging her further down into the darkness.

She suddenly felt warmth and the brittle edges of soft flesh. She gently cupped her hand and scooped the mass from the toilet and onto the floor.

After inspecting it, she became fascinated by its half-formed body – tiny stumps just beginning to sprout from its body, a hint of an ear hole, lidless eyes...

...eyes which gawked in horror.

It suddenly fluttered in her hand – its mouth parted ever so slightly as toilet water dribbled from the corners. Its head slumped; tiny stumps shivered and fell limp.

Mikila searched its flesh for a mouth, then tilted the tiny mass forward, hoping to see it react to her touch. But it only glared lifelessly – its digits curling along with its body as it shuddered one last time and grew still.

Mikila knelt toward where its face was yet to fully form. She stared into its beady black eyes, hoping for some sign of life. She lowered her head and kissed its cold flesh. It tasted of copper and salt, of sorrow and death.

She rose, feeling a steady stream of blood and mucus trailing beneath her. She came to the kitchen and grabbed a Tupperware container and returned.

In her delirium, Mikila could only think to seal the body inside the Tupperware dish and place it in the freezer, preserving it in case the doctors could revive it...or else she could just keep it there and love it like the newborn that it was.

\*\*\*\*\*\*

A great depression ravished her for weeks. She called in sick to work and couldn't even manage to take the container to the doctor. She knew there was little hope and feared that her physician would conclude she was insane and commit her. In that week, she remained curled like a fetus, covers pulled over her head as the sun came and went in what seemed periods of eternity. Even throughout the day, darkness seemed to envelop her, call to her.

She often managed to rise and look at the tiny figure curled inside the container. She swore it had moved one last time after she had placed it there. Or was it just the movement of the container when she had grabbed it? She wished that death weren't so permanent. And she prayed to the darkness that surrounded her. And that darkness answered her.

******

Jeff entered the quiet house and found Mikila asleep. He blew his breath into his cupped hands to see if any of the alcohol still lingered. He felt his erection pounding against his jeans.

He silently undressed and slowly climbed atop her.

During sex, he ravished her and the routine returned once again. He tied her hands and feet to the four bedposts, choking her as he came and rolled away.

When Jeff released her, she clasped the ropes, wrapping them around his neck. She pulled the slack and jerked his head back.

Jeff responded by grabbing the noose and pulling her toward him, smashing her tits against his back.

"I love it when you get kinky," he said, flipping her over as he began pounding her from behind.

******

"Sex always makes me hungry," Jeff said.

Mikila stared hollowly toward the window as rain blew against the glass. A candle flickered madly, projecting Jeff's shadow as an even bigger monstrosity than it actually was.

She watched the shadows play across the walls and realized how one particular shadow looked so miniature and deformed and fragile. It wavered against the door and disappeared.

Jeff shook his head at Mikila and exited the bedroom,

heading downstairs.

He searched the kitchen and tore open bags of potato chips and cookies on the counter. He browsed the refrigerator and slammed the door.

"Chrissakes! Nothing to eat around this place!"

He opened the freezer section and tossed aside TV dinners and bagels until he found the Tupperware container lodged in one corner with ice grown over its edges.

He pulled it out and took the lid off.

Whatever it was inside looked like a piece of barbecued rib, long forgotten. He tossed the container into the microwave and punched the buttons.

The meat started to sizzle and spit fluid after three minutes. Air pockets in the meat whistled as Jeff stared at the smoldering slab until the blood disappeared and the eerie whine of the cooking meat settled to a slight crackle on the plate.

Jeff pranced through the room naked. He stopped to scratch at his balls and hairy ass before sitting at the table with his snack.

"Christ! I could eat this in one bite and swallow it whole," Jeff muttered to himself.

He stabbed the meaty mass with his fork. He heard the same whistling screams the meat had made in the microwave – they grew louder after he pulled the fork out.

He stabbed again and pulled the slab of meat to his mouth. He witnessed a network of tiny blue veins spread across the pale surface of the meat. He wondered what kind of animal it had come from, but didn't care enough to set it aside as he popped it into his mouth...

...and felt something suddenly pinch or bite into his tongue.

He quickly spit the wad out.

The thing plummeted back onto the table as Jeff peered at the pale piece of meat and noticed its beady black eyes.

"Fucking seafood-shit!" Jeff whispered, spitting onto the floor.

The mass on the table suddenly rose and Jeff jumped away from the table.

"Holy JesusMotherfuckingChrist!!! What the —"

The thing stood and bobbed up and down like it was in the middle of some tribal dance. It swung its stumped limbs and maneuvered across the surface of the table.

It lunged off the edge and clung to the hair on Jeff's ass.

Jeff stumbled back and swatted at the thing, but it clung tighter and began inching its way around.

Jeff pounded at his crotch, feeling his stomach ache from the abuse. The thing grabbed his cock and clamped onto the tip of his penis. It began sucking furiously, as if it was starved.

And despite Jeff's fear, he felt his cock grow hard.

But then the pinching feeling returned and he screamed. He reached down and grabbed onto the thing that was latched onto his penis. As he pulled at the lukewarm flesh, he felt his penis being stretched.

He let go and dragged himself over to the counter where the butcher knives were displayed in a wooden crate.

As he picked one out, the thing let go of his cock and scampered up his stomach, to his neck and suctioned itself onto his chin.

Jeff dropped the knife and screamed, noticing Mikila was watching from the doorway.

"Good baby," she said, "Get him!"

Jeff screamed and the thing managed to work its way through his lips and wriggle itself into Jeff's oral cavity. From there it slid to the back of his throat.

His neck bulged. His eyes glazed over with shock as his skin burst open below the Adam's Apple.

A pair of beady black eyes peered from the wound. Its malformed mouth perked in a triumphant grin.

Out of the corner of his eye, Jeff witnessed Mikila approach and probe the wound with her finger. She caressed the thing inside him and drew closer. She flicked her tongue in and out of the open wound, lapping at the thing within.

But suddenly, he felt it depart, its body spreading out inside his, its once tiny limbs feeling as if they were slithering into his skull and branching to all parts of his body.

Jeff tried to scream, but his breath had already been taken.

\*\*\*\*\*\*

The shock on Jeff's face never wore off. He continued to stare vacantly at the walls. His breath remained shallow, his mind an empty capsule waiting to be refilled.

And suddenly, Mikila felt her body changing. She felt alive again. Her breasts began filling with milk, as Jeff became the center of her attention and the only means for which her universe existed.

So Mikila cared for him, bringing his mouth to her breast as he fed often, always returning to his catatonic state thereafter.

Four months passed and he started to kick from time to time. At six months, he flopped around on the floor and exercised his hands and feet. At eight months he rolled over on his back. And at nine months he started to scream.

There was no labor on Mikila's part – no stretch marks or varicose veins or hemorrhoids. The entire development took place inside Jeff's body as his eyes grew dark and his skin sagged in places. The baby took Jeff's functional organs and processed the milk as it penetrated further into Jeff's body and mind. The day of its birth, it connected to the final part of Jeff's body – the brain. And it knew things a child shouldn't know. It became aware of darkness (which had recreated its existence) and despair, of pain and sorrow and emptiness. And it yearned to quickly escape these things.

The man before Mikila now screamed like the infant it actually was. It took to her breast with the intention to feed but with the urge to fondle.

# SICK DAY

Francis couldn't afford to take another sick day. Six straight days and he would surely lose his job.

Francis settled on the toilet, clutching the phone. His sweaty hands trembled, his body itched. He felt as if something was crawling beneath his skin.

He pushed against his silk pajamas, smoothing the wrinkles against his sunken stomach. He watched his belly rise and fall to his breathing until it suddenly bulged outward in the shape of a hideous face screaming from inside him. His stomach gurgled and vibrated.

The sockets in the grotesquely outlined face gradually retracted against his newly swollen abdomen creating two channels delving deeply into the surrounding flesh.

Was this presence trying to suck his matter into its hidden skull or was it simply trying to rip him open so it could unveil its malign self?

Francis patted his stomach. *Probably just last night's chili*, he thought, popping an antacid into his mouth. Swallowing the foam, he felt the face explode against his stomach lining and crawl into his intestines. *And then again maybe it's more than just gas or heartburn.*

"God, I need serious help," he said, staring down in disbelief. "There's something very wrong with me."

Francis pressed the telephone against his face, feeling it

slide and stick to his cheek. The gurgling slowly faded to the recording on the line.

"Hello, you have reached St. Bentley's Catholic Church. Please choose one of the following: If you are calling about service times and collection fees, press one; If you are calling to report an outage of your faith, press two; If you are a pregnant Catholic teenager, press three; If you are late on a personal salvation payment, press four; If you are in need of an exorcism, press five..."

Francis jabbed at the number five button and instantly another recording sounded.

"Welcome to the St. Bentley Catholic Church's Exorcism Office. Sorry, but the office is closed at the present time. Our hours are from nine to five Monday through Friday, closed Saturday and Sunday. If you would like to order a self-exorcism kit which includes holy water and a crucifix, press one; If you are only lightly possessed and would like to hear a recording of one of our priests administering the exorcism vows, press two; If you would like our top ten list on signs that you are possessed by Satan, please press three; If you are in pain from involuntary spasms, the twisting of the head, or from levitation and you have already tried chiropractic care or a heavy sedative, press four..."

Sweat beaded on Francis' brow as he strained, with pants around his ankles, trying to calm his burning stomach.

Suddenly water splashed the sides of the toilet. Strange sounds sputtered, gurgled, then faded. Francis felt the stabbing pain leave his bowels. He stood up, wiping away the slime and blood.

The water bubbled. Francis turned to see a tiny black garden snake slithering up the side of the bowl. The miniature snake slid back down into the water as Francis flushed.

Francis gagged, calmed himself, and peered back into the toilet. "It seems to be getting better," he said while writing the experience down on his medical notes.

Looking into the mirror, Francis noticed his eyes were

glazed, his face flushed, his cheeks twitching madly. He felt his burning forehead as he opened his mouth, extracting his tongue to the terrible taste that had settled there. His tongue rolled down his chin, resting against his neck.

*It must be at least nine inches long*, he thought. Before rolling up his bright red tongue, he noticed the yellow eye glowing toward the back of his throat. It blinked slowly, then disappeared.

In the distance Francis again heard the recording. He lifted the cordless phone to his ear and jabbed at the three.

An upbeat woman's voice erupted: "The top ten signs that you have become possessed are: Number ten.....you woke up speaking a language you had never learned; number nine.....you converse with unseen voices which tempt you to do perverse things like cursing God's name, having premarital sex, eating live chickens, dreaming of having orgies with a clan of demon-faced hookers, carving pentagrams on young children's foreheads, or skipping Sunday School; number eight.....you find that you can move, talk or eat without trying to; number seven....you have impure thoughts about the opposite sex of cold-blooded animals; number six....you have impure thoughts about the same sex of warm-blooded animals; number five....you find that you have developed extra appendages that remind you of a tail, wings, or horn; number four....you find yourself dialing this number over and over again; number three....your daily breakfast consists of a bowl of raw meat with milk; number two....every time you see a cross your flesh withers, blisters, burns, or flakes off; and number one....your favorite color is black or off-white."

Francis sighed, hung up the phone, and smiled at his Chihuahua. "That was really starting to worry me." Francis glanced into the mirror, unable to recall when he had grown a full beard or a double chin. He shook off the strange feeling of someone watching him and smirked. "Thank God I'm not possessed. That would have been really embarrassing going to work like that."

His Chihuahua shuffled next to him. "Probably just a mid-life crisis, *master*!"

Francis agreed. The vision of the bloody axe lodged in his forehead slowly faded.

"You hungry again?"

The silent Chihuahua followed Francis to the freezer, waiting to feast upon the day's scraps.

"You want an arm or leg or what?" Francis inquired.

The dog stared hard at the severed limbs. "If it's the cocktail waitress, I'll take a leg. Exotic dancer, give me a breast."

"So hard to tell." Francis squinted at the severed appendage. "Just take the leg."

The utility room spun around him as his nose popped, pouring out a steady stream of blood.

"That does it," Francis screamed. "Stupid, fucking, good-for-nothing piece of shit body. God damn, Pope-sucking, Jesus-loving fuckers with a medical license can't even cure me, those dick-licking, cum-eaters can shove that fucking stethoscope and "diagnosis: hypochondria" up their money-grubbing assholes!"

Francis gasped for breath, startled at the words that had left his mouth. He turned towards the phone and sighed. "I definitely better call in sick."

Francis glanced at the clock which read: 9:10 a.m. "Boss would fire me anyway, that insane, worthless, moral-preaching, idiot-sonofabitch motherfucker! He always gets edgy when I'm late for a baptism."

# BITCHSLAPPED

The problem with factory life is that there are so many people going nowhere and trapped in the same building all at once. Frustrations build as days are squandered and life dissolves into repetition. Human beings are transformed into numbers that lose precious hours of life to corporate motives and societal trappings.

It's no wonder that I hated Deborah in such an environment. Truthfully, I'd hate her in any environment, but factory life is the ultimate breeding ground for hatred. So being a Jesus Christ-lover-but-I'd-suck-your-dick-everyday-but-Sunday kind of bitch, she was just too annoying and childish and preachy for me to handle. She was a back-stabbing, corporate-ass-kissing, bastard child of the Almighty (*dollar,* that is, though, taking in the way this world is shaping up, the Lord would have to be an even bigger nutball-creator than he or she already is to fuck someone so worthless to give birth to a total waste of flesh such as Deborah).

Deborah was the type of conservative bitch that would prance around and stick her nose in everyone's business, play jokes on others, then scream like a little pissed-off infant when one was pulled on her.

"My goal is to have a picture of Jesus hanging in every room of my house," she said one evening at work.

I smiled secretly, taking her words literally, and envisioning Jesus *hanging* from the gallows in one room, then *hanging* from a light fixture in another. You see, my minds works that way sometimes – call it stress, call it a touch of insanity. It's just how my mind copes with being subjected to this environment, like a laboratory rat running through a maze for cheese, but, for me, I'm working this endless maze for the American dollar, just to be able to survive day to day.

One day I tried to let off a little steam, so I spent the night drawing. By morning, I had finished a dozen pictures of Jesus as a pimp, Sumo wrestler, topless dancer, cab driver, porn star, pirate, mime, ballerina, zombie, plumber, proctologist and crossing guard. I bound them all together and made a yearly calendar and called it "Jesus' Second Comings." The next day at work, I placed them in her locker for her home gallery.

She wasn't pleased.

I was suspended for three days. And my hatred grew.

I tried to push this loathing away and ignore her, but we worked in the same area. And when she started singing gospel songs out loud, I snapped.

At least my hand did.

She smiled at me and I knew what she was thinking, *Ha ha – look who had the last laugh.* And when she did, my hand flattened and arm swung absently through the air, smacking her directly in the cheek.

"Ooowwww! Damn you!" she cried.

Once she spoke, my hand bitchslapped her again.

I just stood there, amazed at how I wasn't able to regain control of my right arm. It felt like a bad dream as everyone around me stared on in disbelief.

"What the hell did—"

My hand smacked her again. A red welt formed instantly across her cheek.

Sweat beaded on my forehead as I tried to hold back my arm.

SHAME RYAN STALEY / 171

"You..." she started.

My arm broke loose again and whacked her again. She stumbled back, then regained her composure. Her lips cracked and a smile suddenly crept forth.

"...are going to be..."

*WHACK...SMACK...WHACK...SMACK.*

Her lip split open and blood trickled down her chin.

"...Fired."

I had never seen a hand move so fast. Like a hardcore pimp, I fluttered my hand back and forth across both cheeks with such lightning speed that she didn't know what hit her. I swore I even heard her neck crack from the violent shaking of her head back and forth.

As she passed out, I had time to actually think about what had just happened. Somehow, my hand had totally branched off from my mind as a separate entity. The only way I could figure it out is that I pushed my hatred so far down that it somehow manifested itself in my right arm and hand. All the anger and hatred had somehow possessed my right limb, causing this violent event to unfold.

Supervisors poured in the room, two of them restraining me. They quickly backed away once they witnessed my hand begin to flutter. Not too long after, two cops showed up and shot my arm off. I served six months in jail and years of probation.

That was the first time it happened.

******

The next time it happened was in a bar. Some guy who looked a lot like an evil Mr. Rogers was taunting my lack of an appendage.

"Hey, somebody stole my beer – I bet it was the one-armed man," evil Mr. Rogers said, followed by a chorus of laughter. Another guy jumped in, "Yeah, somebody stole my wife – the one-armed man did it!" A third idiot finally joined in, "And somebody ran up my tab – it was the one-armed man!"

I'LL BE DAMNED | 172

I jumped off my barstool and evil Mr. Rogers pulled out a knife.

"It's a wonderful day in the neighborhood pub," I sang. "A wonderful day for a knife fight. Would you stab me? Could you stab me?"

"What are you some kind of fuckin' queer or something?" evil Mr. Rogers asked.

"I don't know," I stated, "Bend over and you'll find out."

He didn't bend over. Instead he rushed me. And my left hand came to life and bitchslapped the knife from his grasp. My hand continued bitchslapping him across the bar floor until we reached the jukebox that played some kind of hillbilly trailer trash country song about some whore-bitch that left the singer for another man. Tears and beers and women and a truck, blah, blah, blah — no one really gives a fuck....except three inbred dumbasses in a bar somewhere in ShitTowne Indiana.

My fury peaked and I bitchslapped his head through the entire jukebox display case. Records cracked. Sparks shot across the floor. The crowd cleared to the sound of distant sirens.

The cops finally came in and shot my other arm off. Four years in jail and a lengthy probation followed.

\*\*\*\*\*\*

The final time was just last month. My wife had been sleeping around with another man (kind of like that hick-song playing at the bar that night). I had known for months and suppressed my anger. I was no longer a danger since I had no arms left to bitchslap her silly.

She came home late, drunk as hell, and her zipper was still down, not to mention her bra had mysteriously come up missing.

"Where the fuck have you been?" I yelled.

"None of your fucking business," she said.

"I know you've been fucking around on me."

"Oh really," she said, "What makes you think that? Because I'm not happy and I'm married to a freak who can't even hug me...?"

"Don't," I cut in.

"...Or who can't even satisfy me in other ways. You know, just because you don't have any arms doesn't mean your dick doesn't work."

"Please, don't."

"You do have a tongue don't you? Hell, use your toes if you have to!"

I felt my anger channeling into both my stumps. They flailed, sputtering uselessly.

"I bet I could suck on your dick and you wouldn't even get it up."

She staggered, fell to her knees, and unzipped my fly.

And my cock grew before her astonished eyes.

It poked through my fly and suddenly whacked her across the face. It wagged back and forth, smacking her again and again. I chuckled after seeing my dick-print etched across her flesh. I could vaguely make out the imprint of my cock's head and shaft on her pale cheek.

After the ninth or tenth thrashing, she fell unconscious.

But that wasn't enough. My hatred still burned.

And my dick was still hard, so I shoved it into her mouth. I wiggled it in deeper, lodging it in her throat. Her gag-reflex massaged it instantly. She coughed and gasped, but didn't wake up.

"How you like my dick now, bitch?"

The cops kicked in the door. They took one look at my choking wife and shot my dick off. No real surprise there, I guess. My lawyer said I'm up shit creek for at least ten years. But, by this point, I could care less. What the hell am I suppose to do in society without hands, arms or even a cock besides running in a three-legged race or playing soccer?

But I don't feel safe in here. Especially since I have the most important thing that any man needs in jail: an asshole. And my cellmate, Jimmy, likes me just the way I am.

Helpless and pissed and naked most of the time. I just lay there with my face pressed to the cold concrete, unable to gain my balance and defend myself since I no longer have any fucking arms.

Jimmy's been playing it rough lately – my hindquarters are bruised from his incessant pounding.

My hatred has no limits. Especially since I've learned the one lesson in life that I had rebelled against from the beginning. *What comes around goes around* – no matter if you're right or wrong – life has a way of always bitchslapping you in the end. And right now it's my turn as I'm getting bitchslapped from behind.

But, as life goes, change is the only thing we can count on. And my hemorrhoids have started to grow, creeping forward with every session, reaching out to rip his dick off.

# SHADY ACRES
# CHURCH OF GOD

Some people call it a cult. I call it faith and fun.

There are about 500 of us spread across the field in Shady Acres, ready for mass to begin. It is another glorious Sunday and Reverend Lou begins talking about disco and its modern ties with the Bible. The stripper-nuns are swinging around on poles to each side of the good Reverend with their black and white g-strings and their crosses wedged between their golden breasts.

Sunday mass is a daylong event. I think of it more like a carnival or what the original Woodstock would have been like. Man I love the atmosphere and scenery here. There are children gathered in Sunday school groups, playing throughout the field. One group is swinging at the Jesus piñata with sticks. One boy's shot to the crotch opens the piñata as loaves of bread spill across the ground. Children pile atop one another for the first treat of the day.

Another group of children is playing "Pin the nail on Jesus." And what a sight that is. A teacher spins a small girl around and she heads blindly for the cross. She hesitates momentarily and stabs the nail into the photo of Christ's crucifixion on a poster board.  Ouch!  Christ would've been glad he didn't get nailed *there!*

As Reverend Lou continues in the blue mist of strobe lights and smoke, I watch the new recruits gather near the hot tubs, ready for their baptisms.

Besides the fun, there is also serious faith going on.  The Church has set forth SOS Plans (Salvation Option Savings Plans) for people to save towards getting into heaven.  There's also SPP Plans (Sinner Periodical Payoff Plans) where members of the congregation can pay off their sins weekly and be cleared in the eyes of the Lord.  Lucky for me they accept VISA and MasterCard after the hooker I picked up last weekend.  I'm planning ahead for next month's orgy with some teenagers I know by investing some cash in the Church's SLC Plan (Sinner's Layaway Contribution Plan).  The little sins like greed and lust are reasonably priced, but the big ones like murder cost a lot, so I decided to keep my sinning to a minimum.

Today's Bible history class is this afternoon and we have a big exam over errors in the Bible.  I learned a lot considering that I once thought that God had instructed Noah to include all those animals on the ship.  It turns out that the arc was really just a Loveboat out for a joyride and Noah needed a little variety.  Lucky for him he picked the right weekend to sail since the world flooded over.  The exam also covers popular misconceptions such as that Jesus Christ is always pictured as a white male with a beard when really he's an African American and homosexual too.  And that he was the first of God's bastard children to come.

And God has many of them – more and more everyday.  And I wouldn't call it Immaculate Conception.  Just a few months back, I returned to my tent to find my girlfriend, Daisy, pinned in mid-air at the top of the tent, spread eagle.  She was grunting and panting and moaning, her vagina magically opening and closing like a fish mouth.  Since then her belly has risen, and she has this strange craving for shellfish!  Not to mention her sex drive is suddenly in overdrive.  Praise the Lord!

Pam, the girl in the next tent, is God's whore.  I found this out after noticing she has a birthmark that actually spells the words "God's Whore" across her stomach.  Man, God must be protective when it comes to women (just marking His territory, I guess).  Pam lives by herself and, late each night, I have to go over and unlock her handcuffs and undo the shackles that bind both feet behind her neck.

God must be a kinky motherfucker!  Because one day, I went over too early and was suddenly lifted in mid-air.  My face was suddenly shoved into Pam's small, pointy breasts, and I felt my pants rip off and a hot surge penetrate my rectum.  As Pam dropped, taking my cock in her mouth, God pounded me from behind.

Yes, we are definitely His chosen people.  Hallelujah!

As this week's ceremony starts to break up, the people in the Accelerated Salvation Seminary (ASS) have gathered in a large pit and Kool-Aide is now being served.

Reverend Lou ends his sermon in Jive and the stripper nuns slowly dress as the crowd returns to their tents across the hillside.

Faith flows through my blood and I hate to see this day end.  But there is always Wednesday night mass where each of us is blessed by the holy water that flows through Reverend Lou's bladder.  And I can't forget the weeping statue of Jesus – with his big black Afro and his pink silk robe, we'll kiss his fuzzy sandals and pray that He will always look upon us anew and cherish us as His one and only children.

Amen.

# TWINS

I t was the first time Nathan had really looked at his girlfriend's vagina. It seemed like such a foreign terrain now, like some kind of stretched and mutated alien landscape. Even the smell seemed odd, like she had been bathing in fish oil or douching with salmon cakes.

The whole moment of revelation almost eclipsed the excitement of labor. But Nathan quickly snapped out of it as Jenny screamed, "God, get it out of me!"

"Okay, now push!" the doctor said calmly.

Nathan stared into the dark tunnel as blood trickled out the side. Mucus and water soon trailed as he could almost see her dilating by the minute.

"Okay, I see the head!" the doctor informed them.

Nathan just knelt there, glaring into the dark void that was now eclipsed by a tiny ball of flesh with hair. He dreaded the coming moments, knowing that Jenny was too unstable to become a mom so soon.

******

T he pregnancy was a mistake. Nathan had been seeing Jenny for only six months when they found out the news. Nathan went into a depression after the shock and Jenny was full of excitement and anticipation. Nathan couldn't understand why.

Then came the talk about twins. Jenny was suddenly obsessed with having twins. She told him that she had always dreamed about having twins.

Next came the matching outfits and double strollers. Twin cribs and changing tables.

But the first ultrasound only showed one.

And Nathan thought the madness would end.

It didn't.

Next came a new apartment for the "twins" to grow up in. Jenny wanted something with more space, so that both kids could have their own room. Nathan argued with her, stressed the point of the ultrasound, but it was no use.

"So, it was wrong!" Jenny said. "I'm having twins!"

"But you seen it with your own eyes!" Nathan shouted.

"But I can feel them both. My body doesn't lie to me!"

Nathan felt his anger subside and sadness and pity eclipse everything. He felt sorry for Jenny. He knew she was unstable. Nuts, to be exact, but he couldn't muster the nerve to leave her. Not in her fragile condition. And he couldn't bear to leave his firstborn child to live with a nutcase-mother.

****** 

The baby slid out in a torrent of blood and mucus. It didn't scream. It didn't move.

The doctor flipped it over and slapped its back. Nathan noticed its body was blue, its head was strangely oblong.

Another slap and Nathan heard it cough.

The doctor siphoned the excrement from its mouth and cleaned off its body. He wrapped it in a towel and turned to Jenny, "Congratulations, Mom. It's a boy."

Jenny took it into her arms and cried and Nathan felt his own lip quivering at the sight.

Then Jenny handed the baby to Nathan and started pushing again.

"What are you doing?" the doctor asked.

"My other baby is in there!"

"No. Stop pushing, Jenny. There was only one."

Nathan bundled his son up tight and took a deep breath. The doctor briefly glanced over at him, and Nathan shook his head.

"Please stop pushing, Jenny. You might hemorrhage."

"No!" she screamed, "Get the fuck down there and deliver my other baby!"

"Nurse!" the doctor yelled.

Nathan stared between her legs as a nurse rushed in.

"Restrain her!"

Jenny started fighting the nurse, screaming and kicking. The doctor held her there and managed to work on her stomach, massaging it until a bloody mass plopped out of her. Nathan cringed as the doctor threw the chunk of afterbirth on a scale and said, "That's it, Jenny. I'm sorry but there was only one."

Jenny calmed down suddenly, like the realization finally struck her.

In the middle of the chaos of nurses checking vitals and other nurses administering medicine, Jenny requested that everyone leave her room. The doctor looked again to Nathan, as if to ask why? Nathan just shook his head and was the first to leave. The nurses and doctor quickly finished up weighing the baby, set the IV drip, stitched Jenny back up and turned on the heat lamp where they placed the baby beneath.

Jenny just stared hollowly at the ceiling as each left the room.

When Nathan returned, Jenny had cleaned the blood off the floor and replaced the sheets by herself. She wouldn't speak to him. She just slept.

\*\*\*\*\*\*

A day later, she was still hospitalized. The nurses were monitoring her condition around the clock. She was treated with antidepressants and all sharp objects were removed from her room.

Nathan had to return to work as Jenny's mother watched after the baby.

Around noon, Jenny's mother called the office.

"They're sending her home today," she stated, "The drugs have stabilized her depression and she has really come to terms with it all. She's smiling and joking around. We're packing right now."

"Great!" Nathan said, "I'll meet you at the apartment."

He arrived at the apartment just as Jenny's mother was leaving.

Jenny was waiting for him. She gave him a kiss at the front door and hugged him.

"Where's Daniel?"

"Shhh," she whispered, "He's sleeping."

Nathan smiled.

Jenny smiled back. "And so is Nathan Jr."

Nathan's heart skipped a beat. "What?"

"They're both sleeping!"

Nathan glanced into the nursery to see the familiar sight of two cribs set side by side. He took a deep breath and swallowed hard, fearing that she had somehow stolen another baby on her way out.

Jenny led him by the arm until they entered the nursery. Nathan glanced in on the first crib and saw Daniel curled up and sleeping soundly.

A hollow feeling suddenly pulsed through his gut.

He shifted to look into the other crib.

And his breath caught.

"Christ!" he managed to say. And he closed his eyes. But that didn't make the vision go away.

In the middle of the crib, covered in a tiny blue afghan, lay the bloody remains of her placenta.

Nathan backed away after noticing the bloodstains on the baby mattress and how the piece of afterbirth had shriveled and blackened since he had seen it excreted from Jenny's vagina.

He tripped over the double stroller and crawled out of the

nursery. Jenny seemed not to be phased by his actions. She just stared lovingly over the 1-foot liver-like clump of bloody waste that should have been discarded by the nurses in the hospital.

And he suddenly knew why Jenny had asked the nursing staff to leave so suddenly during the clean-up.

\*\*\*\*\*\*

Nathan tried to talk with her, but the first time he did, she was nursing it.

She had even put a diaper on it.

Nathan cringed, watching her tit wiggle across the hard, cold, blood-encrusted piece of afterbirth. Beads of milk trickled against the side of the mass and dropped to the couch.

"That's a boy, Nathan Jr. Drink Mama's milk, it's good for you!"

Nathan felt his stomach turning.

"You haven't even held Nathan Jr. yet."

She held the blackened bundle toward Nathan and all he felt was pity and sorrow for her. Had he caused her to become this delusional by knocking her up? Maybe if he would have worn the condom, none of this would have ever happened. He loved Jenny and planned on marrying her someday. But now, she had lost all common sense. Guilt slowly flooded Nathan and his sorrow grew.

Once the tiny cold bundle was in his arms, he gazed down at the surreal scene. He could see tiny vein-like clusters branching from the afterbirth. When he looked at it in a certain direction, it almost resembled a baby. A really fucked up baby, but a baby nonetheless.

"Give your son a kiss." Jenny urged.

Nathan complied just to keep her calm. He lowered his lips and kissed the cold flesh-like lump. It tasted briefly of copper and salt. He gagged. Took a breath. Then threw up.

\*\*\*\*\*\*

Nathan's parents were expected to arrive any minute.

He paced the floor as Jenny was changing Daniel's diaper and was readying herself to change Nathan Jr. as well.

*Holy shit*, Nathan thought. He had planned to sneak into the nursery the night before and take the piece of afterbirth for a long ride. He was planning on telling Jenny that Nathan Jr. had been stolen. But then she would call the cops. They would surely take her away and he would be stuck with Daniel and he had no idea how to take care of an infant yet.

"Come here, honey!" Jenny called "Look! Nathan Jr. has got his first messy diaper."

Nathan closed his eyes and started to laugh, madly.

He went to the changing table and saw what Jenny was pointing to. But, of course, it wasn't a turd. A rotted piece had just broken off the mass and fallen into the diaper. Jenny smiled, using the wet wipes on it, smearing dried blood all over the place. She replaced the diaper and tossed the old one in the Diaper Genie.

The doorbell rang.

Nathan had to stall. But he heard the door open and his dad yell, "We're here. Where's my precious new darlings at?"

"Did he say 'darlings'?" Nathan said to himself. He knew right away that Jenny had called them without him knowing it.

Jenny handed Nathan the shriveled body of his so-called son and walked with Daniel in to greet them. Nathan stayed behind, hearing a dog bark in the living room. *Oh God*, he thought, *they even brought Spot along.*

His mind spiraled; his body shook. But then he began to smile for the first time since the birth.

He laughed harder, glancing down at the oblong piece of placenta lodged in his arms. "Gootchie, gootchie goo," he said, tickling it, then he doubled over, pain shooting through his stomach as he tried to muffle his laughter. He envisioned Daniel growing up alongside his placenta-brother. Playing baseball in the backyard. Nathan Jr. in the outfield as birds swooped from the trees, pecking off crusty chunks of his body. He thought about going to King's Island where Nathan Jr. couldn't ride the roller coasters since he was only a 1-foot tall piece of rotten flesh. He thought about the first day of kindergarten, the unlucky girl set up on Nathan Jr.'s first blind date and, of course, all the immunizations he'd have to go through in order to get into school.

Visions struck at Nathan as he grabbed the pacifier from the dresser and shoved it into the half-rotten mass of a baby. The rubber nipple penetrated the shell as blood oozed across Nathan's hand. A putrid stench wafted to his nose.

He laughed harder and said, "This is fucked up, Junior!" He held the piece of placenta in the air, level with his face. "Daddy's sorry, but he's not going to live like this. Your mother's a psychotic bitch and you're just a fleshy piece of rotted innards. So fuck you both!"

Spot barked in the living room again. And Nathan suddenly had an idea.

He whistled, then heard Spot's dog tags come rattling into the nursery.

"Here boy! Got a little treat for you," Nathan said as Spot sat in front of him.

Nathan peeled the diaper off the afterbirth and dropped the crusty mass onto the floor.

Spot circled it, not knowing what to think. He jumped at it, then barked. Finally he dove into the mass and shook it wildly until dried, crusty portions broke off and flew against the wall. As Spot bit deeper, he discovered a moist center. Strings of mucus-blood sprayed against the blue walls. The dog clutched the half-rotted clump of placenta and began chewing, ripping the center apart.

Nathan just stood there and watched, laughing out loud as the dog swallowed hard.

Even when Jenny entered the nursery and released a bloodcurdling scream at the sight of Spot's new chew toy, Nathan's laughter only grew.

Nathan couldn't stop laughing. And the scary thing was that it wasn't the least bit funny. He knew his mind had taken a turn for the worse. But at least that was the end of the twins. No more masquerade that a second child existed.

Jenny had somehow left the nursery and managed to convince Nathan's parents that Nathan Jr. was ill and they would have to come another time. But, strangely, she kept Spot.

Nathan curled under the bedcovers. He didn't care if she killed Spot. It would be the least of his worries at this point. He was exhausted from laughing madly and from the stress of having to watch his girlfriend turn into some kind of lunatic. He rocked back and forth beneath the sheets, blocking out the rest of the world until sleep came.

******

Jenny woke him around midnight.

"Nathan Jr. wants to sleep with you," Jenny said.

Nathan lay paralyzed with fear under the covers.

He felt Jenny pulling on the sheets beside him. Before she departed, she said, "Now don't roll over on him."

Nathan hoped it was all a nightmare. But when he surfaced from the covers and focused through the darkness, he could feel something beside him. And it wasn't cold this time. It was actually warm.

He felt through the darkness and his hands reached under the sheet beside him.

His heart raced.

And he finally felt the origin of warmth.

His hands touched the warm surface that suddenly squished between his fingers.

And suddenly, he smelled dog shit wafting through the bedroom.

# WORMS

Mom had to be a psychic or something. She always knew what was best. Like the time she told Dad not to use radioactive materials in our basement with his chemistry set. Sure it's dangerous, but what were the chances it would actually harm us? And then she started with me.

"Don't let that damn cat in the house. You'll get worms!"

The stray had been mewling outside my window each night. During the day, I'd sat a saucer of milk out for it and sometimes scraps of food if Mom wasn't around.

It was raining like mad the night I opened my window and let the cat in. Once the cat was nestled in my blankets, my mother yelled from the kitchen, "And remember – don't you go letting that worm-infested cat in the house!"

The next day the cat was gone. It had gone back out the window sometime in the night, but left me a present at the end of the bed.

A steamy pile of shit.

The smell of cat shit hung thick in my room. It was only a matter of minutes until Mom's senses picked up the intruding stench and my ass was grounded for a week. I quickly readied myself to cover the pile up, then noticed the little, white worms slithering in the feces.

****** 

For days, I looked at myself in the mirror. I monitored my bowel movements. By the end of the first week, there were no signs of worms.

Then at supper one night, I was lazily combing through my pile of meatloaf when I saw Dad shoveling it down like usual. As I glanced in his direction, I saw one. It was dangling off the side of his meatloaf. At first I thought it was gristle, but after it wiggled, I knew for sure.

Dad finished off the fork full as the worm caught in his teeth. Every time he smiled, the severed end of the worm would flick left and right. I prayed that Mom wouldn't notice and luckily she didn't.

But then one morning, I rose earlier than usual, before Dad went to work, and noticed there was no cereal. I trudged down the hallway and entered my parent's bedroom to ask where Dad had hidden the new box of Corn Pops when all hell broke loose.

Inside their bedroom, I caught my Dad screwing the hell out of my Mom. His hairy ass was pumping like a piston as my Mom's legs were wrapped around his back.

That's when I noticed the giant worm hanging out of his ass.

"God, Harold, I don't remember you ever getting into it so much!" Mom said to him.

The worm did the wave in mid-air, sliding back inside Dad's rectum and he responded by pumping even harder.

I threw up for almost an hour after seeing that. It was a shock itself to walk in on my parents lovemaking session, but then to witness the horror of the parasite being a caboose to that hideous train, was far too much for one kid to handle.

****** 

They kept growing and multiplying after that. Fluffy, the family cat, would drag them behind her as they clung to her

I'LL BE DAMNED / 188

ass. Dad was always scratching at his rectum. And even Mom kept complaining of a massive yeast infection that was coming on. The cat's litter box became a sand-pool for the damn worms.

Mom quickly found out one day after changing the litter. She didn't directly blame me, but kicked the cat out of the house. Days later, I found Fluffy in the backyard. Her gut had burst open, her asshole torn to shreds and her brains had been devoured.

Things were getting complicated.

Especially after they penetrated Dad's basement office, where the radioactive chemistry set was hidden.

Dad was oblivious to their presence one night when he went down to experiment. The next thing I know, I hear a piercing scream. Both Mom and I ran for the basement and there was Dad with a giant worm pulsating from his ass.

It seemed to be growing by the minute, its pale body becoming thicker, tearing Dad's asshole wide open. Its head poked through and curled around, finding Dad's mouth. Now one end protruded from his ass, the other had disappeared into his mouth.

The doorbell rang.

"Goddammit!" Mom screamed, then approached the giant worm. "How the hell are we going to get this sucker out of you?"

My dad's muffled voice couldn't be understood.

"Hold on for a second...somebody's at the door!" she stated calmly.

As Mom walked up the stairs, Dad really freaked out. Though his voice was muffled, I could still make out him saying, "Come here you fucking bitch, get this thing out of my ass!"

I just stared at Dad's chemistry set and noticed the green and yellow stick that pulsed brightly inside a beaker of liquid.

Mom came back downstairs and I heard extra footsteps.

As I peered up the steps, a Jehovah's Witness followed Mom with a handful of pamphlets.

"Right down here. I'll let you talk to my husband about your faith."

The bald-headed religious man took one look at my Dad and started praying. And just as soon as he started rambling off Jehovah's name with a steady stream of rubbish, the worm poked its head from my father's mouth and looked strangely at the guy.

I think the worm was annoyed just as much as we were.

Within seconds, it had exited Dad's body and coiled around the Jehovah's Witness.

Mom's laughter filled the basement, even eclipsing the man's shrill screams.

The worm excreted a vile yellow pus-like stream on the guy's head and shit a green chunk of radioactive goo on all his pamphlets. My father, still weak and recovering, managed to even shout a few cheers.

Pretty soon, the worm ate his Bibles and crawled up his ass.

I don't know how all fifteen feet of that beast fit inside the guy, but it did. Must of have been all that extra soul space he had been mumbling about when he first came down the stairs.

The guy stared, vacant-eyed, as he calmly exited the house. It was as if the worm had taken over his mind.

We left the house and called in an exterminator. Actually several, after the first three died on the job. Finally we managed to rid our house of the parasite.

\*\*\*\*\*\*

From that incident, I should've learned my lesson. But my teenage years came and rebellion followed.

Just a couple of weeks ago, Mom said, "Don't you be dating that girl! You'll get crotch crickets!" She had found out that Lindsey Porter had asked me to the prom.

Prom night came and I found myself in the back of my car, six inches deep in Ms. Porter. She bucked and clawed and fucked my brains out for hours.

Now crabs and herpes I could see, but Mom had to be joking about crotch crickets, I thought. If she would have said, "You'll get AIDS!" I probably would've passed. But crotch crickets!

Mom's a fucking psychic or something. Now I lay in bed tonight and it's dark in my room. And I swear I hear chirping in my underwear.

# BLESSED IS HE WHO TRUSTS IN THE LARD

## 1.

Outsiders claim we're a cult. Others say it's a fat farm. I know it's the last step toward heaven and that we're the chosen.

I was born in Beefleham, on a small farm where my father raised pigs and crops. I remember that night when it all changed.

I was only seven when my father ran into the house, his hands bloody, his face scared white. Ma told me to stay put as she left the house. My father led her to the barn.

Moments later, I heard her scream. I ran for the barn and that's when my life changed forever.

A pig's innards were strung across the floor. A pool of blood had spread beneath the tractor. I looked to my mother and father who were both transfixed by the pig's shuddering body.

It wasn't the first time I had seen my father slaughter pigs. He had let me watch, had taught me the ways in which a farmer must sacrifice an animal to feed the family. And the blood didn't bother me, or the pig's body jerking as the last of the blood circulated out of its pale body and onto the hay beneath our feet. But what did bother me was the thing that crawled out of that pig, pulling behind it a mass of fatty tissue.

My father raised a pitchfork above his head and I flinched as the thing crawled closer to my father.

"Kill it, Maynard!" Ma screamed.

But my father's eyes were glazed. Instead of fear, there were only tears as he threw the pitchfork away and knelt to receive it.

Ma's scream left my ears ringing, disturbing even the chaos that had already settled in my mind. I didn't know what was happening. It felt like a terrible dream, one that made no sense, but hinted at a secret meaning which only frightened me even more.

The thing slithered up my father's arm and he stroked it like a baby, cradling it in his arms.

"Pa!" I yelled, "Kill it!"

But nothing registered. Tears continued to stream down his face.

I thought about going for the pitchfork myself, then stopped to look at the thing. It was pale, gelatinous. It appeared as if it were just a lopped off piece of the pig's fatty tissue, but it moved.

I looked for eyes or antenna, thinking it was some kind of parasitic worm, but saw nothing but fat. I had seen cattle and chickens infected with tapeworms and such, but they were miniscule to the size of the thing on Pa's arm. From end to end, it stretched from Pa's fingers to the side of his neck.

The pitchfork came into view once again, and then my father spoke.

"Oh Lord, we thank you for your presence..."

It never said a word. But somehow it was communicating with Pa. You could see some form of understanding light up Pa's face, as if the thing was from *Star Trek* and spoke through telepathy. And my father understood every word.

And somewhere in the moment, I swore it spoke to me. It said: *don't be scared, my child.* And I immediately felt relieved and forgot about the pitchfork.

## 2.

In the beginning, I'm not sure if I believed it was the real Lord.

My family was never religious, but the concept of Jesus and God were still pounded in my head by society, especially when I started school. I kept asking myself if everyone else could be wrong. There were hundreds of religions out there, but no one worshipped such an entity as The Lard. In fact it was absurd to most.

But life had evolved for thousands and thousands of years. Dinosaurs existed before humans. And there were surely other species that preceeded the dinosaur. So how could people assume that God was of the human essence? And that Jesus would come back in human form? What if the Lord and Savior appeared in a more primitive form, such as Lard?

It spoke to Pa every day and I became proud of the man. He was like Moses in the Bible – one of God's first chosen ones.

And Pa spoke of the Lard's wishes. How the key to heaven was in feeding oneself, to gain bulk (a piece of the substance that the Lord was made of) and how the Lard needed sacrifices each month. The Lard also told father how he needed to spread the word. The Lard had come to collect the chosen ones. And it said that the end time was nearing.

I never would have believed these things if it weren't for the flood.

It had rained for three days straight. The creek had flooded its banks and washed into the field. By the third day, the water was threatening our livestock. Pa had moved the pigs to the highest ground, but there weren't many hills.

I heard my father praying that night, "The Lard is my

Shepherd.  It shall lead us through the tough times and guide us to the Promised Land.  Praise the Lard, Amen!"

I thought my father was insane.

But that night I became a true believer that he was the chosen.

The water level crested near midnight.  Half the livestock had perished and the barn where the Lard stayed was washed away.  My father awoke, scrambling after he heard the crack of wood, as the water carried the barn away.

"Oh, my Lard," he screamed, "Where has it gone?"

We waded through the current as rain continued to plummet from the sky.  Gray clouds swirled furiously overhead, blocking most of the moonlight.

And then we saw it.  Where the barn had collapsed and washed away, the Lard remained.  It was not even affected by the raging waters.  In fact, it floated atop the water – a true miracle.  It moved across the waters gracefully until it met Father and I.  And this time it spoke to both of us.  It told us what needed to be done next.  And my father and I both broke down into tears.

## 3.

The property was damaged.  The field was wiped clean of all crops.  The pigs were dead and dying.  We packed up some essentials and were ready to make the move to the neighboring town of Jerusalaham.

I watched from the distance as Mother and Father knelt before the Lard.  My father's tears glistened in the sunlight as he kissed my mother.

The Lard stretched itself out on all sides, to where it had expanded into a perfect circle at least six foot in diameter.  It pulsed and bubbled in a strange ritual just before my father pushed my mother's head into its mass.

I gritted my teeth as the Lard's body formed into a giant hand that clutched my mother's face.  Her scream was cut short as the Lard's body pierced her eyeballs and surged into her skull. Her face distorted as the Lard leeched its way through her pores, crawled into her mouth and nose.

She fell backwards, putting her hands to her face. But her flesh just melted into the Lard's body. Bones fell to brittle ash that was consumed by the pale mass quivering before us.

Her clothes were ripped off as the Lard's tentacles pushed between her breasts and between her legs. Her body arched, as if in ecstasy, before convulsing toward silence.

"Son," Father said, "I know it's hard to understand, but it's the Lard's way and it should be followed. The Lard had told me that women are here to serve men. And, sometimes, after they have served our needs, they need to be sacrificed for higher purposes."

I nodded, trying my best to understand.

I looked back to the Lard, which had grown twice its size. Then I headed for the truck and our new life in Jerusalaham.

## 4.

We quickly found meaning to why the Lard had told us to relocate. Jerusalaham was a quiet farming town, much like Beefleham, but somehow would become the center of our following.

Within two weeks, several men from town had joined Father's Sunday service. They were skeptical at first, but after they witnessed the Lard firsthand, they quickly converted.

During the next seven months, our congregation grew to fifty men. And with this support, the Lard started performing miracles right before our eyes.

First, it was the six-pack of mineral water. My father had placed it into the Lard's body. Its flesh quickly consumed the bottles. Its body quivered and then everything went silent. Its flesh parted again to the sight of a six-pack of beer.

The congregation sat in awe at this feat. If anyone had their doubts up to this day, they had been quickly erased.

The more people who came, the more miracles the Lard

performed in front of its chosen flock.

A bag of potatoes were turned into pork rinds.

The Lard's pale body touched an anorexic teenager. A mere two weeks later she had miraculously gained eighty pounds and increased six sizes around her waist. And she had only eaten but a bowl of lettuce and a Nutra-Grain Bar since being first touched.

Of course, once she was nicely plump, we sacrificed her.

My father began preaching about mass. Body mass.

"True believers must seek what makes one holy."

The Lard touched each member. And each grew in bulk.

But as each of us grew in size, the Lard began to diminish.

## 5.

The Lard had only feasted once in several weeks when the group became restless.

"It needs a sacrifice, Maynard," one of the devoted followers said during mass one Sunday. "It has sacrificed itself for us, for our sins of being undernourished. We need to act!"

Father had told me that the time was near. He told me that there would be great strife inflicted upon us from the outside.

I urged him to make a sacrifice. But we had no women in our group to give. And my father delayed in making a decision.

That night, the Lard called to me. It woke me from my dreams and lured me to our sanctuary in a new barn that was built with money from our Sunday collection plate.

The Lard spoke directly to me. It said, *Jerusalaham is filled with non-believers. And lots of women. Bring two. Then sacrifice them to me.*

\*\*\*\*\*\*

The only time I had ever seen a woman naked was when the Lard had crawled into my mother's cunt. Now I was in a room full of them, swinging on poles and dancing on the laps of old men.

I was indeed aroused, but kept my focus on the mission.

Shortly after arriving, a young blonde straddled me.

"Hi sugar," she said, "haven't seen you around here before."

"First time," I said, feeling her breast push against my chest. I felt my penis rising and wondered what the Lard would think of this indiscretion. But then it spoke to me from afar. It said: Indulge, *indulge.*

"I want to have sex with you," I said.

The blonde just laughed. "You're a straightforward one, aren't you sugar?"

"It's just that I've never been with a woman before."

Her eyes suddenly lit up.

"I'm off in a half hour."

"Do you have any friends you could bring along?"

"Sure do, baby. How's two for the price of one sound?"

I smiled and nodded.

"My name's Monica. Wait for me."

\*\*\*\*\*\*

I had never expected it to be that easy. Within an hour, I was back on the farm with two women on the hilltop.

Moonlight cascaded down Monica's back as she straddled me in the grass. Her stripper friend, Alexa, lay beside me, shoving her breast into my mouth.

Monica was bouncing away as I felt myself quickly come inside her. Pain erupted in my balls and my penis ached from her wild hip movements.

"Where are you?" I whispered.

Monica stopped, but Alexa jumped right on. I thought they were going to drain me completely. But then I saw the Lard's pale body moving up the hillside.

It quickly arrived to save me.

First, it took Monica who rested, watching her friend devour me. I saw it flatten out into what looked like a giant pale, fatty penis. Monica screamed after seeing it come up beside her, but she couldn't run.

The Lard thrust forward into her ass and she fell forward, her breasts smashed against the ground as the Lard pounded her from behind.

"Oh God," she screamed.

She didn't know how accurate that was at the moment. But her scream alerted Alexa who jumped off me and tried to run away. But I quickly grabbed her arm and pulled her down.

I stood mesmerized, watching Monica get fucked from behind by the Lard. I held Alexa against the ground, making her watch as well.

Monica quickly fell unconscious, just as the Lard pulled out, then shot a stream of oily fat across her back, reinserted its body into her cunt and continued to pump wildly.

After it had finished with Monica, it moved to Alexa. I let go of her and she scrambled briefly, but the Lard contracted into a bullet-shaped projectile, which rushed at her from behind, burying itself into her hind end.

There wasn't much pumping this time. Three quick thrusts and the Lard disappeared into Alexa's body. She screamed, then moaned, her body quivering as if in ecstasy. Her back arched, then her skin suddenly split apart at the abdomen. The Lard's body seeped from her pores, collapsing her flesh. Streams of the Lard's body exited through her vagina, mouth, ears, with her bones snapping under the immense pressure. The Lard exited, reuniting its body back into a whole slug-like entity that crawled over the remains once again, engulfing the rest.

I was so enthralled that I hadn't even noticed that Monica had gained consciousness and was half way down the hill.

I leapt, began to chase her, then was called back by the Lard.

SHANE RYAN STALEY / 199

I did not question The Lard when It said to let her go. But I knew the consequences that it would bring about.

My father's prophecy was set in motion.

## 6.

Less than 24 hours later, a mob met my father at the gates to our property.

I watched them arguing, then a man hit my father with the butt of a rifle. Several others returned to their pickup truck.

Within seconds, my father's body was crushed beneath its wheels. The gate was knocked over.

"No!" I yelled, running for the barn. The truck sped toward me, stopped at the entrance.

"Where is it?" a man yelled.

"You don't know what you're doing. It has come to save us."

"Would you listen to this shit?" another man yelled, pointing his gun at my head.

"I will not betray the Lard, the Savior."

His finger started to squeeze just as another man yelled, "It's in here...I see it!"

"No!" I screamed.

But it was too late.

Several men surrounded the Lard, dousing it with gasoline. Two other men held me back.

"The Lard is my Shepherd..." I began.

One struck a match.

"I'm sorry, Lard," I cried.

Flames ignited.

The Lard bubbled and popped. Liquid and oil shot from the heat. It wriggled across the barn floor, but only managed to ignite the straw beneath it.

There was no hope after that.

Everything was charred beyond recognition.

Our sanctuary burned to the ground along with our savior.

# 7.

I fled Jerusalaham the same day, leaving behind the broken remnants of what had become a group of the chosen.

I remember my father's words when he once said, "It is not for us to question the way of the Lard."

But yet I found myself doubting what had happened.

I found myself alone in a world that worshipped false deities. I passed churches every day and saw the crosses. I imagined those crosses replaced with another sign of a gasoline can and a match. But I knew it would never come to be. The world was so blind. They could never accept the truth. So why was I chosen to carry this secret when there was no way I could spread the Lard's message? How was I to tell the world the truth?

When my doubts peaked, the Lard spoke to me in dream. It told me that even though it was gone, its presence still lived on inside me.

I awoke no longer doubting. I felt my bulging belly and I understood.

******

That day I walked the streets, seeing overweight people everywhere. They stopped at hot dog stands to scarf down food. They lingered in cafes. There were so many people living the way of the Lard, but they had yet to really acknowledge it.

It was my mission to teach them.

In a restroom at a fast food restaurant, a fat man came out of a stall. Mustard and ketchup stains lined his collar. I thrust my belly to his and whispered, "I'm here to save you."

He shoved me away. "What are you some kind of queer or something?"

I smiled, then clamped my hands around his buttocks and pulled close to him. I could feel my insides call to him.

They began to bubble and he quit fighting me and let it happen.

My skin parted and a tiny white piece of lard formed, dangling like a phallus until it erected to touch his skin. He peered down in awe as it worked its way into one of his pores and disappeared.

After that, he slowly backed away. Tears formed in his eyes and he said, "Thank you."

For months I continued to spread the Lard across the land. The United States was such a susceptible country to the Lard. So many people practiced the Lard's ways, but didn't even know it. I showed many by transferring the Lard within me, to share it with them.

But I grew more and more weak as days went by. My weight had dropped and I feared I would surely perish.

My father's prophecy claimed there would be a Second Coming of the Lard. And as I prepared more and more of the chosen ones by showing them their faith, I knew the time was nearing.

And suddenly the Lard spoke to me almost ten months from the day it had perished.

*It has begun, my child,* It told me. *Go and meet the rest. The time is here where the chosen ones will rise!*

I traveled a great distance, until I found myself back in Jerusalaham. The Lard led me to the hospital, guiding me to the second floor where I met the members of my father's congregation. Besides that group, others flocked in, even some I remembered encountering in bathroom stalls and parties. Each had grown since I last saw them; their bulk was wild and free as I had dwindled, feeling as a disgrace to the Lard.

But then I felt saved. I had sacrificed myself for a higher purpose. I knew this while looking through the glass to the maternity ward and seeing Monica being wheeled into a room.

She had gained a considerable amount of weight and her stomach was round like a melon.

Doctors and nurses rushed into her room as my people crowded around the door.

Peering in, I saw the head coming out. It was long and pale, threading its way out of her vaginal canal.

I rejoiced, knowing that it was only a matter of time until the world knew the real truth.

It was finally our time to rise.

I'LL BE DAMNED | 204

Shane Ryan Staley is the editor of *Delirium Magazine* as well as editor and publisher of both Delirium Books' hardcover and paperback line. He has also authored two recent chapbook collections, *Chocolate Jesus and Other Weird Perversions* (Delirium Books) and *Sick Days* (Eraserhead Press), and has appeared (or will appear) in numerous small and semi-pro magazines such as *The Edge: Tales of Suspense, Earwig Flesh Factory, Black Petals, The Urbanite, Terror Tales* (online), *Strangewood Tales, Horrorfind.com, Outer Darkness, The Reaper, The Black Abyss, Blood Coven,* and *Frightmares.* He won the 1999 Killer Frog Contest with his short-short story "The Mailman" and was runner-up in the short story category with "The Boy With Razor-Sharp Teeth." He has been working on several books through Delirium, including *Dark Testament,* an ultra-controversial Biblical horror anthology set for release in January of 2001. He resides in Warsaw, IN with his wife Christi and sons Lane and Dylan.

Despite what's been said before (both by his enemies and himself) **Brian Keene** is not the devil incarnate, an ex-terrorist writing under an assumed name, the Generation X leader of the Illuminati, or the Pope. He is the author of books like *No Rest for the Wicked*, *More Than Infinity*, and co-author of *4x4* (along with Michael T. Huyck Jr., Geoff Cooper and Michael Oliveri). He is also the creator of the award winning *Jobs in Hell*. His website, **http://www.briankeene.com**, contains household decorating tips and several favorite recipes.

**R. S. Connett** is one of the most influential underground artists in print today. His website, **http://www.vomitus.com**, contains a vast amount of his works to date, including paintings, line art, t-shirts and written words about his artwork by the artist himself.